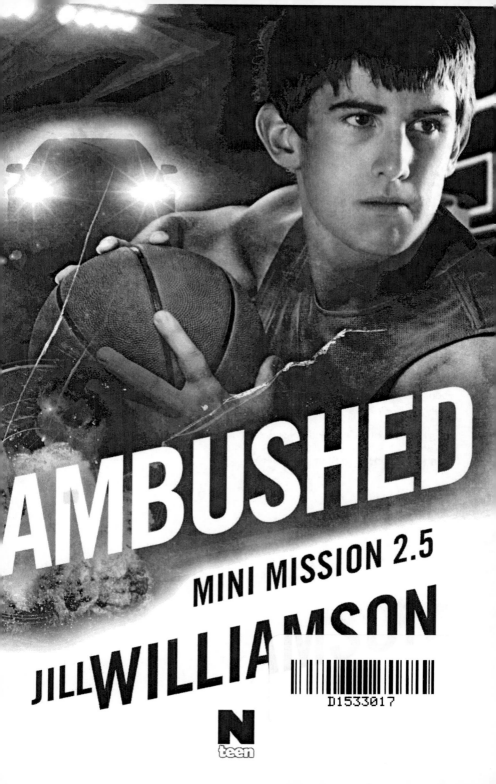

AMBUSHED

MINI MISSION 2.5

JILL WILLIAMSON

N teen

Scriptures taken from the Holy Bible, New International Version®, NIV®. Copyright © 1973, 1978, 1984, 2011 by Biblica, Inc.™ Used by permission of Zondervan. All rights reserved worldwide. www.zondervan.com. The "NIV" and "New International Version" are trademarks registered in the United States Patent and Trademark Office by Biblica, Inc.™

The author is represented by MacGregor Literary Inc. of Hillsboro, OR.

Cover Designer: Kirk DouPonce
Editor: Rebecca Luella Miller
Character Sketches: Keighley Kendig
ebook design: Kerry Nietz
Mission League Logo and miscellaneous images: Jill Williamson

International Standard Book Number: 978-0-9887594-5-9

Printed in the United States of America

Other books by Jill Williamson

The Mission League series

The New Recruit

Chokepoint

Project Gemini

Ambushed

The Blood of Kings trilogy

By Darkness Hid

To Darkness Fled

From Darkness Won

The Safe Lands series

Captives

Outcasts

Rebels

Stand-Alone Titles

Replication: The Jason Experiment

Nonfiction

Go Teen Writers: How to Turn Your First Draft into a Published Book

Alpha Team

Gabe

Spencer

Grace

Wally

Diakonos Team

Nick

Isabel

Arianna

Lukas

Restricted Access

YOU HAVE ACCESSED THE
INTERNATIONAL SERVER FOR
THE MISSION LEAGUE

THESE FILES CONTAIN CLASSIFIED INFORMATION
ON THE ORGANIZATION, AGENTS, CRIMINALS, PROCEDURES,
TRAININGS, AND MISSIONS

GOD HAS CALLED. YOU HAVE ANSWERED.

CLASSIFIED MISSION BACKGROUND REPORT

TITLE: Previously in My Life . . .
SUBMITTED BY: Agent-in-Training Spencer Garmond

IN CASE YOU'RE COMING INTO THIS adventure in the middle, a year and a half ago I was recruited into the Agent Development Program of the Mission League, a secret branch of INTERPOL, whose primary objective is to follow the will of God in collecting, analyzing, evaluating, and disseminating intelligence against the rulers, authorities, powers of this dark world, and the spiritual forces of evil in the heavenly realms.

Yeah, I know what you're thinking: churchers. And I thought the same at first. But then I found out that my real name is Jonas Wright and I'm in a witness protection program of sorts, hiding out from my criminal dad, who was responsible for my mom's death. Real nice, huh?

So I went on a training mission to Moscow. And I met this woman, Anya Vseveloda, who was working with the Russian mob to get people hooked on drugs and into a cult called Bratva. I'd been having dreams about her for years, and I found out I was gifted in prophecy.

When I got back to California, Priere showed up—he's the official intercessor for our group of agents-in-training. He told me that I matched the profile for a sixty-year-old prophecy and that some bad guys were after me because of what I did in Moscow. Agents started following me everywhere to keep me safe. The baddies guy-napped me after Homecoming last year, but the agents nabbed them right back.

Things quieted down for a while. Then last summer, I went to Okinawa, Japan, on another training trip. I got my first red card—a real assignment—to follow this girl. I botched it, of course. And she led me to Anya (bad chick from Moscow), who accused me of being the Profile Match and wanted to know who the First Twin was. Like I had a clue. I managed to get away, but in doing so, Anya cut me across my chest and I had to get stitches. It's actually a pretty sweet scar.

Now I'm home again and totally focused on basketball. Coach did some research on the NCAA recruitment process, and, let's just say, I've got a lot of work to do. But I'm starting to become a bit of a celebrity in Pilot Point.

Oh, and there's another Light Goddess movie coming out soon, so I'm curious if this one has the same creepy similarities to the Bratva cult as the other one did.

So that's what's been going on. I'm sure you're ecstatic to have learned all this. If you really want to know how everything works out, it's all in this report.

Spencer Garmond
Agent-in-training
Pilot Point Mission League

REPORT NUMBER: 1

REPORT TITLE: I Stalk a Hot Blond
SUBMITTED BY: Agent-in-Training Spencer Garmond
LOCATION: Harris Hall, The Barn, Pilot Point Christian School, Pilot Point, California, USA
DATE AND TIME: Wednesday, December 21, 6:14 a.m.

I YAWNED AND LOOKED AT GRACE'S EMPTY desk for the sixteenth time that morning, then read the next question on the Outdoor Survival Training final exam:

16. In the Mission League, S.E.R.E. stands for
a. Survive, Evade, Resist, Extract
b. Survive, Evade, Resist, Escape
c. Survival, Evasion, Resistance, and Escape
d. Survival, Evasion, Resistance, and Evasion

The Air Force S.E.R.E. had the word "and" in it; the Mission League one didn't. And I was pretty sure "extract" was from the UK version. I circled *b*.

Yes, Mr. S gave finals. And, yes, they were hard. Plus they counted on my transcripts, a fact I learned this fall when Coach taught me the rules. Turns out, the NCAA had strict requirements for high school students who want to play NCAA college sports and receive a scholarship at the D-I level. My grades weren't bad, and the glorious Mission League had helped me out with two years of required foreign language that I'd never realized I was getting credit for. Nice, right?

My biggest worry had been my SAT scores. Until I'd found out that the NCAA had a sliding scale to average my test scores with my GPA. With that formula, I was in pretty good shape for most schools, except maybe Berkley, Stanford, or USC. I didn't want those schools, anyway. I wanted UCLA.

Honestly, as long as I could get a power school in a power conference . . . Well, that was the dream. And I even had a few offers to prove that I wasn't delusional. Life was good.

My life, anyway.

I looked at Grace's empty desk again. After following her around all semester, I still hadn't found out who was hurting her. And she'd ignored all my direct questions. But every time she was absent, she came back the next day with a bruise.

I had a feeling that the truth might be the only way to get her to open up. But I really didn't want to say, *Hey, Grace. I dream about you.* I mean, how creepster was that?

I read question 17 and scribbled in the answer as best I could.

17. Fill in the following acronym:

S _Size up the situation_
U _Use my senses_
R _Remember where I am_
V _Vanquish fear_
I _Improvise_

V <u>Value my life</u>
A <u>Act like the natives did</u>
L <u>Live by using my head</u>

Another glance to her empty desk.

Why did I keep looking? Did I expect her to show up halfway through the test?

18. If someone is suffering from hypothermia, you should give them
a. cold water; b. brandy; c. warm tea; d. ginger ale

I would have said *b*, but I could still hear Arianna's lecture after the customs agent took my bottle of saké wine I'd tried to bring back as a souvenir from Japan. I had told the customs agent I needed it in case of hypothermia on the upcoming snow training trip. But Arianna told me that drinking alcohol might make you feel warmer as the blood-alcohol level rose, but it actually lowered the core temperature of your body.

I circled *c*.

Occasionally, Arianna's lectures came in handy.

Since this was the Outdoor Survival Training year in the Mission League, there would be no international summer trip, but we were going to camp in the snow for a few weeks. So far, we'd spent the fall semester learning how to tie knots, what to pack that might save our lives, and how to do first aid—the Resusci Annie practice dummy is ugly, and she reeks. I'm just saying.

Next semester was to be hands on adventures. We'd get to go hiking, build fires and shelters. And then the snow camping trip. I was pretty excited about it.

I looked at Grace's empty desk. Would she be with us then?

I muddled my way through the rest of the exam and left the underground bunker. The air was chilly outside, but December in Los Angeles didn't require more than my hoodie. The sun was just now rising, making the Verdugo Mountains look black.

I was a few minutes early for school, so I got my stuff out of my locker and went to homeroom where I could text Grace.

It wasn't too early for a text, was it? Grace went to Pilot Point High School. They started about the same time as we did.

My classroom was empty. Not even Mr. Moore had arrived. I took my seat in the back and pulled out My Precious II from my hoodie pocket.

Yes, I had a new iPhone. It had taken a few weeks. And Priere had said I didn't deserve it after losing mine in the Pacific Ocean, but to my incredible luck, it wasn't his call. The head honchos wanted me to have it so they could track my every move.

I tried not to think about that most days, and I was *so* happy to get another iPhone.

What should I text? Everyone had been teasing me about stalking Grace. They all thought I liked her. But I just needed to figure out who was hurting her. That was all. I swear. I didn't need more girl drama. I had really bad luck with girls.

I typed, *You okay?* into the keypad.

"I can't believe you finished the test before I did."

I looked up from my cell. Arianna dropped her bag beside her desk in the front row.

Mission-Ari, as some kids called her, was slim and plain,

though she'd started plucking her eyebrows this year. Or waxing them—whatever girls did. And her top lip was peach-fuzz free. I gave credit to Isabel, whose mother owned a salon.

Arianna was still Arianna, though. In her continued protest against the knee-length skirts that were part of the girl's uniform at our school, she'd been given permission to wear whatever navy blue skirt she wanted. Today's was a fluffy floor length one that looked like mosquito netting.

As she made her way down the aisle toward me, the fabric got stuck in the book rack of one of the desks. The whole desk dragged after her for a few steps. She turned back and growled, then pulled her skirt free. "Oh no! It tore!" She shot me a pout like I should feel bad for her or something.

"I'm sorry?" I said.

She dropped the hem. "No worries. I can fix it. Hey, are you coming to youth group tonight?"

Over the past few months, in my attempts to rescue Grace, I'd become a full-fledged churcher at Cornerstone Christian. I still hadn't said the hocus pocus prayer. I don't know why I was dragging my feet. As much weird stuff as I'd seen, I didn't doubt the thing worked. Maybe I was just being stubborn.

You think?

"Can't. I have a game," I said.

"You had a game last week."

"I know, but . . ." A yawn snuck up on me and rendered me speechless. Once I'd recovered, I said, "I'll be there next week. But not the week after. Grandma and I are driving to Arizona the week of New Year's."

"Hey, Spencer, my man." Chaz fell into the seat next to mine and offered me his fist. I tapped it. Arianna rolled her eyes and drifted back toward the front of the class.

Chaz, who could pass for Paul Walker's son, had cropped his blond hair so short he almost looked bald. "You text Coach Warren yet?" he asked me.

"Will you stop?" Chaz and his dad had been all over me about going to USC. Grandma and I had gone down there on an unofficial visit two weeks ago, but I didn't know. USC's program wasn't the best. And they couldn't seem to keep a coach. I hadn't gotten the feeling that their staff had been all that thrilled to meet me either. Plus it was South LA. Shudder. "I don't think I want to live down there, man."

Kip sat down in the seat on my other side. "Not when he could live it up in New Meh-hi-ko."

Here we go again. "There's no way, Kip," I said.

"Stop with the negativity. Just get your grandma to drive you over there after Tucson."

"That's an extra *thirteen hours*. I already have to be in the car with her for fourteen." Being poor sucked. Big time. But so far I didn't have any official prospects that looked like they might fly me and Grandma in for a visit, not that I could take any official visits until I was a senior, anyway. But Coach said we shouldn't wait to check things out. Hence the drive to Arizona to visit Arizona State and the University of Arizona. Both of which were Pac 12 schools that had shown interest in me.

"Come on," Kip said. "You have to go to New Meh-hi-co. It's ranked third right now."

"I thought you wanted to go to Duke." Desh fell into the seat in front of mine, blocking my view of . . . everything, really, except for his massive back.

"They didn't respond to my tapes," I said. "Coach says I'm too far down the pipeline for them. The Wildcats are my best bet right now."

Kip heaved a long, dramatic sigh. "Whatever. It's your career."

"A player like Spencer would be a star at USC." Chaz spoke to Kip right through me, like I wasn't even there. "If he goes Lobos, he'll be on the bench for *at least* two years."

"You don't know that," Kip said. "If their center declares for the draft, they could suck next year."

"Then why you trying to get Spencer to go there?" Chaz asked.

"They won't suck if Spencer goes there," Kip said.

"Spencer's not a center."

"Doesn't matter. If their center goes NBA, their starters will transfer."

My phone buzzed. I pulled it out. Grace. My heart did a little flip until I saw her response.

Yah.

What did, *Yah* mean? Did she mean, *Yeah?* Like, *Yeah, I'm fine. I'm alive and not hurt?* Or, *Yah, m fin but cant spel cuz I hv brane damaj?*

Kip and Chaz were still arguing: one on each side, me in the middle. Story of my life these days.

Since I was little it had been my dream to play college basketball and later in the NBA. And I'm good enough too, for the NCAA, at least. But I had no idea what a mess all this recruiting business was. And when I got back from Japan and made up with Coach for ditching his summer program, he told me he'd been learning how to get me scholarship offers. My life changed that day. If I wanted this—and I did—I had to grow up, get serious about picking a college. Coach helped me register for the NCAA Clearinghouse and started sending my

7

DVDs to schools. He even helped me make my own YouTube channel so we could post my highlights there.

And it worked. Once the contact period opened, Coach started getting interest calls about me; a few schools had even offered early. And local reporters were always trying to talk to me—to see if I'd made a decision yet.

The NCAA had a million rules about how these things had to go down to keep coaches from trying to bribe me. Sadly, there were no rules that kept my friends from giving me their advice. And Chaz and his dad were the worst.

I used to pine over Duke, Syracuse, and Michigan State. I now knew I wasn't going to any of those programs. Power schools tended to recruit closer to home unless I got ranked as a five star, which was unlikely since being at a small school and not playing AAU ball meant I had very little exposure. And since I lived on the West Coast, it wasn't likely I'd get offers from an ACC or Big Ten school, at least not the ones I wanted.

At this point, if I could play for a power school in any power conference, I'd be happy. So far my only prospects in that department were from Arizona, Arizona State, and Gonzaga, but I was still holding out for UCLA. Grandma and I had visited them too. I liked their coaching staff. Plus they were always on TV, had won plenty of championships, sent lots of guys to the NBA, and I considered them the home team.

Now, if I could only get them to offer me.

• • •

There was no League after school today because of finals, so I ran over to Pilot Point High to check on Grace. I stepped into the old gym and was greeted by sneakers squeaking on wood and girls' chanting voices.

Hey! Hey! Let's do it again!
Everybody yell, GO, FIGHT, WIN!
Go, Fight, Win! Do it again!
Go, Fight, Win! GO, FIGHT, WIN!

The loud sounds put me more on edge. *Please let her be here. Please.* I scanned the gym and spotted Grace on the far left. She seemed okay. She was jumping and doing all the motions along with everyone else. I released a slow breath.

"Spencer!" Jasmine Jacobs ran up to me and gave me a hug that smelled like the middle of Macy's.

Megan and Kip and been trying to set me up with Jasmine ever since school had started, and I'd caved and asked her to PPH's homecoming back in October. That had ticked off Kip. He'd wanted me to bring her to *our* homecoming, but I'd wanted to go to hers so I could keep an eye on Grace.

I know. I was pathetic, huh?

But I'd asked Jasmine as a friend, and their whole team thought I loved Grace anyway, so of course it had all worked out to my ultimate embarrassment. Grace had come with Justin Rutherford, a guy who played football for PPH and was the preppiest jerk since the cast of *Jersey Shore*. I didn't think they were going out, but I wouldn't be surprised if he was the one hurting her. I needed to figure out where the dude lived.

"Hey, Jaz," I said, but I kept my eyes on Grace. Was that a limp or had she just stumbled?

Jasmine poked me in the ribs, which kind of tickled. "Why haven't you texted me lately?"

I stepped away from her, not wanting to be distracted

until I knew Grace was okay. "You want me to text you?" I had no idea what to say to that. Why wouldn't she go away?

"Yee-ah." She slapped my chest and yelled, "Grace, your boyfriend's here!"

That got my attention. "Don't do that," I whispered, but Jasmine just giggled and yelled again. "Gracie Lou Who, your boyfriend's here for you!"

Across the gym I heard Grace mumble, "He's *not* my boyfriend."

Story of my life, really.

I paced for ten minutes, wearing a groove into the floor, until practice ended and Grace finally came over.

She had that look on her face, like I was some stray dog she couldn't figure out how to lose. "Hey, stalker."

"Hey, tumblelina. You missed class this morning." I took in every millimeter of her face but couldn't tell if she was wearing more makeup than normal.

"Checking up on me again, huh?"

"Naw, I just wanted to say hey." And see if there were any bruises on your face. I shifted to get a better look at the back of her neck. The lighting in here was pretty bad.

"Spencer, look. I like you. But I'm not ready for a boyfriend right now. I'm just . . . there's a lot going on."

That comment pulled my eyes to hers. My face got all hot. She didn't understand. She thought I was just trying to hook up. "I don't want to be your boyfriend. Just your friend." And keep you from getting beat up.

"Even my best friends don't come to my cheer practices."

That was fair. "Well, you didn't show this morning, so I was worried about you."

She folded her arms. "Why are you always worried about

me? I might not be able to bench my own body weight like you, but do I look like an invalid?"

"No." It was time to tell her. Spill my guts and hope I didn't look like more of a freak than she already thought I was. "Okay, this will sound weird but . . ." I swallowed. "Well . . . uh . . . you know how last spring when you joined the League and Mr. S made you take that spiritual gifts test?"

"Yeah. I got service and teaching."

"Okay, good. That's great. Well, I got prophecy."

"Oh." Her eyebrows sank. "Wow, that's . . ."

"Yeah. And that means that, uh . . . sometimes I, uh, I know things. Well, I, uh . . . I see them, sort of." Smooth. Did *I* even know what I was talking about?

She cocked one eyebrow. "You see them."

"Yeah, in my head." I tapped my temple.

She folded her arms and sank into that "prove it" pose girls do so well. "And what have you seen, Spencer?"

I looked at the floor. "I've seen you get hurt."

"How? I fall at practice or something?"

"No." I scratched the back of my neck. "Some drunk guy. He uh . . ." Yup. She was looking at me like I was a freak. This wasn't going how I'd planned. "They usually come true, Grace. The things I see. Not always, but . . ."

She just stared at me. No expression on her face, but I could have sworn her eyes got misty. But maybe that was just the bad lighting. "Well, I'm fine, Spencer." She smiled, a nice big fake one. "No one hurt me, okay?"

Liar. "Okay."

"So stop following me around."

"Okay." Yeah. Like *that* was going to happen.

11

REPORT NUMBER: 2

REPORT TITLE: I Have a Sleepover with a Hot Blond
SUBMITTED BY: Agent-in-Training Spencer Garmond
LOCATION: Dino's Pizza, 235 3rd Street, Pilot Point,
California, USA
DATE AND TIME: Wednesday, December 21, 8:12 p.m.

THAT NIGHT'S GAME WAS A BLOWOUT in our favor, which put us at 10-1 for the season so far. The reporter from the *Pilot Point Bulletin* was waiting to talk to me after, which did take long. No, I hadn't made a decision yet. No, I didn't know when I would.

Once I got away, Grandma and I went out to pizza with Gabe's family, who'd come to watch my game. All seven of us crowded around a half-circle booth in the back of the pizza place. Grandma, Mr. S, Kerri, Gabe, his twin sisters Mary and Martha, and me. Though the twins were identical, they were easy to tell apart by their personalities and the way they dressed.

Oh, and one of them thought she was going to marry me.

I'd known Mary had a little crush on me since my trip to Moscow, but when we got back from Japan last summer, she told me we were going to get married someday.

Yee-ah. Middle school girls, anyway.

Gabe and I had turned it into a game, joking that I had to get at least a dozen goats before he'd be willing to part with his sister, since that's what men did a zillion years ago. So when I'd seen a little stuffed goat in the mall last week, I bought it for Mary for Christmas. I thought it was funny.

"Mary, I have something for you." I dug the goat out of my backpack and tossed it across the table.

She caught it and sucked in a delighted breath. "It's a goat!"

Gabe snatched it from her. "Oh, no. Goats go to the brother, not the bride. I keep the goats."

"Goats go to the father," Mr. S said.

"Give it back!" Mary tried to take the goat from Gabe.

He held it up in the air. "You still owe me eleven goats, Spencer," Gabe said. "One isn't going to be enough."

"I just thought she could take care of the little guy until I got the whole herd together," I said. "Plus I liked its beard."

"I want to see its beard!" Mary grabbed the goat's tail and pulled. Gabe readjusted his grip on the thing's head. "Don't you dare break him, Gabriel!"

"Gabe, give your sister the sheep," Mr. S said.

"It's a goat," Gabe said. "And it's rightfully mine if Spencer thinks he's going to marry her." But then he let go, and Mary flew back against Martha in the restaurant booth.

"Ouch!" Martha scowled at Mary, then Gabe, then me.

But Mary straightened, smiling, and snuggled the little goat. "I'm going to name him Ramzy because he's going to grow up to be a big ram."

"Goats aren't rams, Mary," Martha said.

"Thank you for the present, Spencer." Mary beamed at me. "I know you think I'm just a dumb eighth grader, but when you're twenty-seven and I'm twenty-four, things will be different. Trust me."

Okay, she was getting weird again. I probably shouldn't have encouraged her. "Yeah, I'll be playing for the NBA."

"That's *not* what I mean," Mary said. "You and I will—"

"*Mary,*" Mr. S said. "That's enough."

"Sorry, Daddy." Mary set Ramzy in front of her plate and tugged on his little beard.

The whole thing would be pretty funny if Mary wasn't gifted in prophecy like me. There was no way for me to know if she was just being a goofy middle school girl or if she'd seen something.

I was glad Mr. S had ended the conversation.

After dinner, on the way out to the car, Mr. S pulled me aside. "Spencer, I was hoping you'd be available to come to a special birthday event I'm having for Gabe. It's not something he knows about, so I'd appreciate it if you kept it to yourself."

"Sure, when is it?"

"December thirty-first, pretty much all day. You'll be home in time for dinner, though, in case you have plans for New Year's Eve. I checked the basketball schedule before I picked the date in hopes that you could come."

"Really? Thanks, Mr. S." But an all day party? What was *that* about?

"It's important that he have some of his friends there," Mr. S said. "Think you can come?"

As serious as he was looking, I wondered if Gabe was going to get some national Boy Scout award or something. I checked my phone and entered the date into my calendar.

"Yeah, I can be there."

"Thank you, Spencer. I really appreciate it. I'll get you the details later. And remember, it's a surprise."

"Sure, no problem."

• • •

When I got home a little after nine, I had another Facebook message from my dad. He'd contacted me when I got back from Japan, then started messaging me on Facebook. He didn't use the name Alex Wright on Facebook, which was the name I *think* he was born with. He was Ving MacCormack online. Said he'd changed his name years ago. I hadn't accepted his friend request or answered any of his messages yet. I clicked open his latest.

> Nice triple-double tonight. You guys blew them away.
> Dad

Uh . . . Had he been at the game?

When I'd first gotten his letter, I was ticked. I mean, Officer Kimball, my Mission League handler, had told me my dad was a traitor who'd gotten my mom killed. But I kept thinking about how Anya had planned to cut me—to try and force me to fit the attributes of the profile match prophecy. What if my dad had been trying to do the same thing for himself, and all that traitor stuff had been an accident?

I could relate to that kind of accident.

In his letter, my dad said Grandma wouldn't let me see him. So I hadn't told her about the letter or his Facebook messages. I hadn't told anyone. I was torn. Because what if the

Mission League misunderstood what had happened? What if I had a chance to know my dad, but the Mission League wouldn't let me?

I didn't know what to do. I needed to find out the truth before I made a decision, but so far I had hit nothing but dead ends.

I opened my intercession journal to the most recent page. I wished I'd have a prophecy about my dad. That, I could use. I didn't know what to do with all this Grace stuff.

Date	Type	Concerning	Description
Dec 2	Dream	Grace	Riding in a car with a drunk man. Fighting.
Dec 4	Dream	Grace	The one when I find her hurt on the floor of her room. *see pg. 16
Dec 5	Dream	wolves	The one where wolves are chasing me. *see pg. 1
Dec 8	Dream	Grace	Grace runs down a hallway from someone. Shuts the door and locks it. A man pounds on the door. Tells her to open up. She climbs out the window.
Dec 12	Dream	woman	The woman having a baby in the cabin. *see pg. 2
Dec 14	Glimpse	Grace	The one where someone is shaking her. *see pg. 12
Dec 16	Dream	Grace	The one when I find her hurt on the floor. *pg. 16

I'd tried spending more time with Grace in hopes I'd have another glimpse, but she'd been avoiding me lately. Telling her about my dreams probably hadn't helped matters.

So I loaded up Planet of Peril on my MacBook and put in my earbuds to listen to some music. Kip had already logged on, so in a few minutes Kardash, my bounty hunter, was flying in a plane with Kip's pilot Badios.

We were in the middle of an expedition to the Gorganan Mountains when My Precious II bleeped.

Text message from Grace: *Look out your window.*

My heart back-flipped. I pulled out my earbuds and stood from my desk. The curtains were closed. I carried my cell phone to the window and drew back the blue fabric.

Grace was standing outside, two feet from the glass.

I just stood there. Struck stupid. She motioned to me, mouthed words: Open the window.

Duh, man. Move it.

I dropped the curtain and tossed the phone to my bed, then kicked some dirty laundry under my desk just in case she looked inside. My room had been in far worse shape. Today Grandma had been in here. Put clean sheets on my bed and made it.

I loved the woman so very much just then.

I closed my intercession journal and put it in my desk drawer, then went to my window. I hooked the curtain into the little fabric loop and pulled up the old-style window—the house having been built in the 70s. I hadn't opened the window since it had gotten cold, and the frame stuck a little on the paint, but thankfully I got it up. How dumb would it have looked if I couldn't get my own window open?

But I did. And then I stood there. Staring. Until I noticed

the black streaks on Grace's cheeks. Makeup. She'd been crying.

My stomach roiled with dread. "What happened?"

"Can I come in?" Her voice croaked. She was still upset.

"Yeah, uh . . ." I glanced at the wall that separated my room from the living room, wondering where Grandma was in the house.

"She's in the front," Grace said. "I can see her sitting in a chair doing something with yarn."

"Crocheting," I said, offering her my hands.

Instead of taking them, she shrugged off a pink backpack and pushed it at me. I took it and set it on the floor. When I looked back, she'd hoisted herself up and was climbing inside.

I stepped past her and shut the window, then pulled the curtain closed. Last thing I needed was neighbors telling Grandma they'd seen a girl climb in my window.

Holy figs, I had a girl in my room! I hoped it didn't stink. I didn't know what to do or say, so I just stood there. She'd have to say something eventually, right?

But she didn't. She wandered slowly into the room, studying the basketball posters on my walls, the things on my desk. I got nervous then, wondering if there was anything I didn't want her to see. I spotted a pair of boxers on the floor by my door. I ran past her and kicked them under the bed. Then I locked the door.

Grace looked at me then, her eyes wide and bright blue. "You going to keep me in here for good?"

If I could, yes. "I just don't want Grandma to come in. She doesn't always knock."

"She wouldn't like you having a girl in your room?"

I shook my head. More like she'd cancel the trip to Arizona

and ground me until I was eighteen.

My phone bleeped. Kip texting me: *Where r u?*

Oh, the game. I texted back: *Grandma*

"I didn't know where else to go," Grace said, her voice whining a little like she was going to start crying.

I swallowed and searched her face. "Are you hurt?"

"I'll live."

I didn't like that answer, but she had climbed through my window without help, so nothing could be broken.

"Have a seat," I said, motioning to my desk chair.

But she sat on the bed. My bed! What did *that* mean?

"Can I stay here tonight?" she asked.

"In my room?" I said it without thinking, and my eyes had gone cartoon-wide. Of course that's what she meant, or she would've gone to the front door. But just seeing her sitting on my bed had taken my imagination places I didn't need it to go right then. Whoa, boy.

"If you don't want me to, it's okay," she said. "I can call Arianna or Isabel. It's just . . . I don't want to tell them why and you already . . ." She looked at her hands.

I already knew. "Are you sure you're okay?"

She shrugged one shoulder. "I might have a bruise or two, Spencer, but I'm fine."

Bruises.

I wanted to hurt whoever had hurt her. I gritted my teeth and made myself calm down until I could speak without sounding like an angry lion. "Was it Justin?"

Her eyebrows arched up on her forehead. She had perfect skin. Not a blemish. "I thought you knew who it was." Then she laughed, a silent laugh that was all breathy. "Justin . . . No, it's not Justin."

Then why hadn't she gone to his place? "Does Justin know?"

"Nobody knows but you."

Oh. Well, me and whoever saw my intercession reports, but I wasn't going to say anything about those. Why make her mad?

"So can I stay?"

Gee. Let's see . . . Gorgeous girl wants to have a sleepover with me? Yes or no?

"Yeah." I turned around and opened my closet a crack to make sure nothing came falling out. I grabbed my sleeping bag from the top shelf and turned back to Grace. She was pulling off her hoodie. Underneath she had on a white tank top. Hello. Gorgeous girl undressing on my bed.

I forced my gaze to my computer. The *PoP* instant messenger screen had popped up and there was a long list of messages from Kip.

21:49 [Badios]: dude, can you tank?
21:49 [Badios]: i'll help you.
21:51 [Badios]: where r u? tank, man!
21:51 [Badios]: hellooooo?
21:53 [Badios]: did she kick u off?
21:54 [Badios]: text me when u can

"Sit down," Grace said. "You're so tall, it's making me nervous."

I jerked my knee toward my bed but stopped. Maybe I should sit on the chair. Grace was like a toddler standing on the court in the middle of a Warriors/Pacers game. I needed to make sure she didn't get hurt, even by me.

But she patted the bed beside her, which settled the matter. I sat down, holding the sleeping bag on my lap, inhaling her coconut smell, and searching my suddenly empty brain for something to say.

I came up with, "Why didn't you tell Arianna or Isabel?"

"It's embarrassing. Would you want to tell people?"

"I guess not. But they're your friends." Her little golden cross necklace was all twisted. In a very bold move for me, I reached out and turned the cross until it was facing the right way. It was a crucifix, though, not a plain cross. It was on backwards, and now Jesus was looking at me.

I'm being a good boy, I told him, then dropped the cross and looked away to prove it.

"I wear it that way on purpose," Grace said. "I like Jesus's face looking at my heart."

I glanced at her. "Are you Catholic?"

"I *was.* In Miami. Here I go to church with Isabel and Arianna. It's different from going to mass, but I like it. I like both."

"How'd you meet them when you go to PPH?"

"When we first moved here, my mom went to their salon and got to know Isabel's mom. She had us over for dinner."

"And you got to know Lukas too." Grace had dated Isabel's little brother last year.

She looked at her hands and bumped her arm against mine. "I don't want to talk about Lukas."

Good. Me either. "What do you want to talk about?"

"I don't know. What else do you have dreams about?"

I didn't want to talk that. "Nothing but you for a while now. It's not just dreams. Sometimes they're glimpses, which means I see them when I'm awake."

21

"Really? That's weird."

"Yeah." Tell me about it.

"Jaz says you're obsessed with me. Said you only went to homecoming with her to spy on me."

I studied the knot on the strings holding the sleeping bag in a roll. "I was *worried* about you."

"Because of the dreams?"

"They're pretty intense. It's like I'm there. I can even smell the beer."

"You probably think I ask for it, huh?"

Was she nuts? "I don't think anybody asks for that."

She looked at me then, like *waaay* into me. Her icy blue eyes were intense and had tiny flecks of orange, right around the pupil. I think she could see my thoughts because her gaze shifted to my lips. That made me look at her lips, but then I got really nervous and all I could do was stare. I imagined leaning down, kissing her, her kissing me back, the awesomeness of—

A sudden knock at the door, Grandma's gentle tapping.

I dropped the sleeping bag, which rolled over in the corner behind the door. I also might have had a massive heart attack.

"Spencer? I'm going to bed."

I clutched my knees and took a deep breath. "Okay. Goodnight."

The doorknob rattled. "Open this door, please."

Mother pus bucket . . . I stood. Grace did too, running for my closet. Well, at least one of us was thinking straight. She shut herself inside, so I unlocked the door and pulled it open.

"Yeah?" Don't look guilty. Just look normal. Look calm.

"What's the matter with you?" Grandma asked.

"What? Me? Nothing."

She barged past me into the room. "You've been playing

that game again." She stopped at my desk and glared at the computer screen, hands propped on her hips.

"You didn't say I couldn't."

"Do I have to say you can't do things in order for you to know you shouldn't do them? You're sixteen years old."

I thought of Grace in the closet. "Uhh . . ."

"It's a violent game, and I don't like it."

"Okay." So, was she telling me not to play it anymore? I thought about clarifying, but if I didn't, I'd have that loophole going for me if she caught me playing again. Right?

"It's after ten o'clock on a school night. What finals do you have tomorrow?"

"Chemistry and English."

"Get some sleep." She walked back toward the door. "And turn that computer off."

"Yes, ma'am."

"Goodnight, Spencer."

"Night."

She pulled the door shut behind her, and I locked it, fingers trembling.

Way too close.

I stood there a moment, staring at the closet door, thinking about what I'd wanted to do before Grandma had interrupted. I needed to be smart here. Kip would tell me to take advantage of the situation. But I had a feeling that if I kissed that girl, she would put my heart in her pink backpack and carry it around. She would own me. When a girl owned me, I forgot to think. And I couldn't afford to be stupid with Grace's safety on the line.

I walked to the closet and pulled open the door. "She's gone," I whispered.

Grace came out and picked up the sleeping bag.

I took it back from her. "You take the bed. I can sleep on the floor."

She offered me a small smile. "Thanks."

It might have been fun to stay up late and talk or play cards or something, but Grandma had said lights out. And this wasn't the night to test the woman's patience.

I unrolled the bag and waited for Grace to get under the covers. I grabbed my phone, which had another text from Kip: *she kill u?*

I texted back: *No. Gotta go to bed, though. Finals.*

Then I shut off the lights and used my cell to see while I burrowed into the sleeping bag.

Could I sleep? No way. I just lay there staring at the ceiling, watching the headlights move across the walls every time a car passed by outside, thinking about the beautiful girl lying in my bed, head on my pillow. Maybe it would smell like coconuts tomorrow. If it did, I'd have to make sure Grandma didn't wash—

"It's my dad," Grace said. "He drinks too much and sometimes hurts us. That's why my parents separated. Dad moved out here to get sober. Mom and I stayed in Miami. But he talked her into giving it another try, and it *is* better. But . . . he's still sick."

Sick. She said it in a sad way like the man had cancer, but I heard it in the angry way like the man should be in jail.

"Would you like me to kill him?" I asked. "Or better yet, have Wally do it?

She snickered. "No."

"Would you like me to kick his—?"

"No!"

"Shh!" *Please don't let Grandma come again.*

Right. Like God was going to help me out with this one.

"Sorry," Grace whispered. "I don't want you to *do* anything. Or tell anyone. This is me and my mom's problem, Spencer. Not yours."

Well, I guess that settled that.

Not really.

REPORT NUMBER: 3

REPORT TITLE: I Get Ranked by Recruiting Coaches
SUBMITTED BY: Agent-in-Training Spencer Garmond
LOCATION: Grandma Alice's House, Pilot Point, California
DATE AND TIME: Thursday, December 22, 5:27 a.m.

I WOKE TO THE BEEP, BEEP, BEEP OF a dump truck backing up. A cool breeze tickled my ear. I rolled onto my back and propped myself on one elbow. Open window. Curtain waving in the wind. Dark outside. No sign of the pink backpack on the floor by the window, which meant . . .

I sat up to find my bed empty, the blankets pulled crookedly over the mattress like she'd tried to make it in three seconds. I checked the time on my cell—5:27.

There was no morning League today because of finals; we'd taken ours yesterday. So I inch-wormed my sleeping-bagged body up onto my bed to sleep another hour.

My pillow smelled gloriously of coconuts.

• • •

Arianna found me in the hallway before my chem final and

pulled me aside. "Grace stayed the night at your house?" It was an angry whisper, like the whole thing had been my idea.

"What? Are you getting prophecies now?" I asked. "How do you even know that?"

"She texted me this morning to ask if she could get ready at my house. What's going on? She wouldn't tell me."

"Then I'm not telling you either. That's up to her."

"Spencer! Don't be like that?"

"Like what? Not a gossip?" That should get her. Arianna was always telling Isabel not to gossip.

She pursed her lips, thinking. And it didn't take her long to find another way to chastise me. "You should never have let her stay in your room. It was inappropriate."

"What would I do without your daily lectures?" Live a happy life, that's what.

"You need someone to remind you who you are. I think you forget sometimes. Too much time spent in the company of Kip and Megan, perhaps."

Personal foul. "Nothing happened, okay? I slept on the floor. I was the perfect gentleman." In action, at least. My thoughts, however . . .

"It was still inappropriate."

"Sorry. Next time I'll leave her on the street." Yeah, right.

Arianna punched my arm, which hurt about as much as me getting hit with a balloon. "You know what I mean. You should have told your grandma."

"Look, I've been trying to help Grace all year. I wasn't about to scare her away by squealing to my grandma. Give me some time to figure this out, so I know how to help her."

"If she's in trouble, you should tell someone."

"Yeah, well, thanks for your two million cents. If you're

done, I've got a chem final to pass." By the skin of my teeth.

"Spencer . . ."

I walked backwards for a few steps. "Ask Grace, Arianna. It's her business to tell, not mine." Then I turned around and walked to the chemistry classroom.

Grace had asked me not to do anything to her dad or tell anyone. I was going to honor that. For now. But that didn't mean I couldn't check out the guy sometime.

My chemistry final sucked. I hated walking away with the feeling like I'd flunked the thing. I wasn't too worried for basketball, but anything less than a *C* in the class, and I'd have Grandma to deal with. Thankfully I wouldn't find out how I did until spring semester started, which was after the Arizona trip. So I had that going for me. Which was nice.

I was free until lunch, so I texted Grace to see how she was—no answer, of course—then I went to play basketball with some of the guys out back. By lunchtime, I'd received a heartfelt response from Grace: *Im fine.*

I'd always thought it was guys who replied in two-word answers. Why couldn't I get this girl to talk to me?

Lunch today was "breakfast for lunch," one of my faves and a nice touch to end the year. I sat with Kip and the guys.

"Dude, did you see this?" Kip pushed his cell phone at me.

It was a page on the Light Goddess website that had a full image of Brittany in her sexy demon battle outfit on one side of the screen. I read the header. "Join the Jolt Revolt."

"It's a promo for *Jolt IV: Daystar*. You can host your own Jolt Revolt party, and if you get at least fifty people, they'll send you a free screening copy of the DVD."

"Really?"

"Yeah, but they track the email addresses, so people can

only sign up for one party. You're coming to mine, okay?"

"Sure."

Nick Muren sat down at the end of our table with his thick friend Jeb. "When you going to do yours?" he asked Kip.

Kip narrowed his eyes. "Why?"

"Well, I figure if we pick different days, we can make it so everyone can go to both."

"We have to get fifty unique emails each," Kip said.

"No problem," Nick said. "If you need some emails, just ask. My dad has a whole prayer chain full that we can use."

I snorted. "I'm sure the prayer chain will be thrilled to get emails about a *Jolt* movie."

"Shut it, Spencer," Kip said. "I might need extra emails to qualify."

So Nick and Kip started making plans for their Jolt Revolt parties, and I just sat there wondering why Nick was being nice to us all of a sudden.

I'd been so preoccupied with Grace that I'd never found out why Nick had gotten kicked off the trip to Japan this past summer. I glanced at the round tables on the side of the cafeteria where couples usually sat—Kip and Megan didn't believe in couple segregation. But Gabe and Isabel were over there. They'd finally started going out just before homecoming, much to my delight—I was sick of hearing Gabe whine.

I'd have to ask Isabel about Nick. But I didn't think she'd ever told Gabe about her "Nick mission," so I'd have to catch her later or something so I could ask when Gabe wasn't around.

Easier said than done. Finding Isabel and Gabe apart was almost as hard as finding Kip and Megan apart. At least Gabe and Isabel weren't making out all the time. Knowing Gabe, they were probably saving that for marriage.

• • •

I'd thought about buying a Christmas present for Grace, but with her already thinking I was a stalker, I decided not to push my luck. Christmas was on Sunday this year, and Grace wasn't at church. I texted her *Merry Christmas*. She didn't reply.

Gabe and Isabel were inseparable that morning, so I couldn't ask Isabel about Nick. On Monday and Tuesday, our basketball team had the Beverly Hills Tournament, which we won. And I earned an all-star medal and the MVP trophy.

I know, right? I hoped UCLA had been watching.

That Wednesday at youth group, I still couldn't get Isabel alone to ask about Nick. Grace wasn't there, which had me a lot worried until Arianna shared a prayer request for Grace and her mom to have safe travels coming back from Miami where they'd gone for Christmas.

So that answered that.

After youth group, I finally broke down and asked Lukas for Isabel's cell number.

The next day, I called her. "You know how hard it is to have a conversation with you when Gabe's not around?"

"I like having him around," Isabel said, her Latina accent thick as always. "Why do you want to talk to me without Gah-bree-el, anyway? This about his birthday party? I don't know nothing. It's only for guys."

What? He was turning eighteen and couldn't have a co-ed party? I shook off the bizarreness and focused on my task. "No, I've been wanting to ask you about Nick. Do you know why he didn't come to Okinawa?"

"Es-pensor, you know I'm not supposed to say."

"Yeah, but I already know you were assigned to watch him, and he's acting all weird right now. I don't trust him."

"Well, it was nothing to do with those strange friends who kidnapped you," Isabel said.

She meant Blaine and Tito. They were in prison, as far as I knew. "Please, Isabel? It could be important." Which wasn't true. I was just being nosy. But where Nick was concerned, I justified this as taking preventative measures to protect myself.

"He got in trouble for drugs, okay?" Isabel said. "He almost went to jail. The judge gave him drug court instead but wouldn't let him leave the country."

What an idiot. "What drugs?" It had to be pot.

"I don't know. I didn't find out that part."

My phone cut out. I looked at the screen. Text message from Kip: *chek ur fb, man!*

"Okay, thanks, Isabel. I won't tell anyone."

"You better not, Es-pensor."

"I *won't*." Girls, anyway.

I ended the call, then pulled up Facebook and found a message from Kip: *dude! check it out!*

And there was a link that took me to a webpage for ESPN Nation Basketball that had a profile for me. It had my picture, my stats, school, hometown, and position. And it had a star ranking of three and overall ranks for my position as a point guard, my ranking in the state and in my region.

No way! No way!

I already had four FB likes. Sweet!

Wait. Was I really only a three-star player?

But I was ranked twenty-five in the state of California for the point guard position. That had to be good, right?

I tapped "like," shared the link on my FB page, then called Coach and filled him in.

"You're a four star player," he said. "If you're patient that ranking could change. It probably won't, though."

"How could it change?" If I was a four, I wanted a four on the site.

"Well, the longer you hold out, the more chances coaches will have to see you play or to see your game tapes, which means you'll get more ratings. And I've been thinking you could maybe play AAU next summer."

Really? "I thought you didn't like AAU."

"I don't, but if it will get you exposure . . . We could get you on a team that's going to the Super 64 in Vegas in July."

Vegas? "But I promised I'd be with our team this summer." I'd ditched last summer to go to Japan.

"You know my off-season program is to work on skills," Coach said. "We're training for fall. Getting ready for the season. That's why we don't do summer league. It's not about winning games in the summer. It's about improving individually so we can win games during the season. But you need to do what will get you the most exposure. An AAU team *can* get you more. It might not, but it could."

I had mixed feelings about AAU ball. "Who's the coach?"

"There are lots of coaches. I know a guy who'd put you on his team. He's not going to help you improve, but he'll give you a fair chance to play. Look . . . AAU is a selfish game, Spencer. At your level it's about showing off what you can do for anyone watching. Playing with them next summer won't help your game, just your exposure to college coaches."

I only needed more exposure to UCLA. "What if I commit to Arizona and then UCLA offers?"

32

"Won't happen. You commit now, UCLA will back off. There are a lot of players out there at your level, and you giving Arizona a verbal commitment shows UCLA that you're happy with Arizona."

"Could I go to Arizona as a freshman, then transfer?"

"You could, but it's not likely. Transfers are pretty complicated, from what I understand."

My brain sort of blanked then. I didn't know what to do. If I wasn't in the Mission League, I might be able to handle playing AAU. But I'd exhausted myself last year trying to keep up with everything. Adding an AAU team just might kill me.

"You don't have to decide this minute," Coach said. "It was just an idea. You could do way worse than either Arizona or Gonzaga."

"I know." They were all good offers. I just didn't know what to do.

"At least wait until after your trip to decide anything. Seeing the schools might help."

Doubtful. I'd already seen UCLA, and I wanted it. But maybe after seeing Arizona and Arizona State, I'd want them too. It was probably a good thing I couldn't afford to fly up to Gonzaga. Then again, there was no rush. If I waited until my senior year, maybe some schools would fly me in for an official visit.

But how would I decide then?

• • •

Former Mission League agent-in-training Jake Lindley called to say he was picking me and Lukas and Wally up at eight in the morning on Saturday for Gabe's guys-only party.

"Kind of early for a party," I said.

"It's not local. We've got to drive up past Lake Hughes."

"Why?"

"Because that's where the party is, fool."

"You still driving that Ford Ranger?" I asked.

"Of course."

"Then I call shotgun." I'd once folded myself onto one of the jump seats in that tiny pickup. I wasn't doing it again.

Jake just chuckled. "Yeah, we'll see."

But thankfully when Jake showed Saturday morning, Lukas was already tucked into the back behind Jake's seat.

Jake's perfect cornrows hadn't changed, but he was wearing round glasses now. He was pre-law, so maybe he thought they helped him look the part. No bow tie today, though.

And this year Lukas had ditched the faux hawk and had been wearing his platinum hair blown back big over his head. He still dressed like a punk.

I climbed into the front seat. "No Wally?"

"He's getting a ride from his mom. Refused to ride in the jump seats," Jake said.

"Oh yeah. He says he can only ride in the front of a vehicle." Which I thought was a crock. "How's Stanford? Can you just pick up and leave whenever you want?"

"I drove down for the weekend," Jake said. "Gabe's my boy. And I wanted to be here for him."

"It's just a birthday party," I said. "Couldn't you send a card?"

"This is more than a birthday party, man. Mr. S has been doing these for Gabe since he was fourteen."

"Oh-kay . . . you're freaking me out. Where exactly are we

going and will there be animal sacrifices involved?"

Jake chuckled. "Funny. Naw, it's like a . . . How can I put this? Like a mini men's retreat."

Lukas leaned between our seats. "Like a church thing?"

"Kind of," Jake said. "But for us to be there for Gabe."

Oh. Yay. I suddenly felt as if I'd been duped into something. Mr. S had given me plenty of lectures since I'd known him. And "mini men's retreat" sounded like a lecture party to me. Whee. "Why didn't Mr. S just say that?"

"Does it matter?" Jake asked. "Maybe he didn't say cuz he knew you'd freak out and not come. Don't tell me you're freaking out?"

"I'm good," Lukas said.

But I wasn't so sure.

The "Gabe becomes a man" lecture slam was held at a rustic camp center called Pine Canyon, an hour and a half north of LA in the middle of nowhere. Jake parked the truck, and we all got out. The place was pretty desolate. Sagebrush and dirt, just like every other SoCal mountain.

Jake headed across the dirt parking lot toward a large cabin with windows all across the front. I followed, kicking up dust with every step. Lukas walked alongside me. It was chilly, but the clear sky promised a warm day.

"So, what'd we get ourselves into here?" I asked Lukas.

"Don't know. If it gets bad, I'm not opposed to stealing Jake's truck. We'd just need to snag his keys."

"Did you bring any hairspray?"

"Ha ha. And no, I didn't."

"Too bad." Lukas was a ninja with an aerosol can in hand.

We entered the cabin, which was a cafeteria of sorts filled with round tables. A window/counter on the left wall peeked into a kitchen.

Gabe was sitting at a table with his dad, Wally, and Pastor Scott, the youth pastor at Cornerstone Christian. Pastor Muren—Nick's dad, who was the head pastor at Cornerstone—sat nearby. Then five other old dudes I'd never seen before.

"Hey! It's our celebrity athlete," Pastor Scott said.

Yeah, that was me. Hometown celeb. Whoop whoop.

"And that's the last of them," Mr. S said, smiling at us. He nodded toward the soda machines lining the right wall. "If you guys want to get yourself a drink, then join us at one of these tables, that would be great."

Would it? I wasn't convinced. But I helped myself to a root beer, heavy on the ice. Lukas got a Pepsi and four straws, and we sat at an empty table behind Gabe's.

Mr. S stood up and clapped his hands together. "Thanks for coming, everyone. Many of you have been here from the start. You mean the world to Gabe, and I'm thrilled you took the time to attend this final celebration. I felt it was important to invite some of Gabe's peers this time. With the exception of Jake, they're all younger than he is, and this day will give him a chance to do for them a little of what you've done for him."

I wiped a drop of condensation off my cup, not sure I wanted to know what these old dudes had done for Gabe.

"Spencer, Lukas, Wally . . . on Gabe's fourteenth birthday we kidnapped him and brought him here. We put him through a host of challenges to mark the change in his life. Gabe became a man that day."

Wait. A guy was a man at fourteen? Since when?

"Each year since, I've given him assignments," Mr. S said. "On his fifteenth birthday, I asked him to write his own definition of what it meant to be a man. Gabe, will you share what you wrote?"

"I call it the three Rs," Gabe said from his seat. "A man is respectful to himself and others. He's responsible for his words and actions. And he strives to be righteous in all he does."

"Amen," Pastor Muren said.

Yep, this was a church party. I raised my eyebrows at Lukas, who took a long drink from all four straws at once while Mr. S went on to explain how he had Gabe write his own dating rules. Then Gabe shared them with us.

I'm not making this up, I swear. And it *did* explain why Gabe was president of the Prude Patrol and not just a member.

"When he turned sixteen," Mr. S said, "I wanted Gabe to learn to manage his own journey of faith and growth. So I asked him to discern where he was in his walk with Christ, what his weaknesses were, and come up with a plan to take care of his own needs. Will you tell everyone what you learned?"

A loud slurping noise turned my attention to Lukas, who was finishing off his soda in style. I wasn't the only one looking. Lukas had everyone's attention. I stifled a laugh.

"Sorry," Lukas said, pushing his empty glass aside.

"Go on, Gabe," Mr. S said.

"Okay, well, I made a list of my weaknesses, and Dad had me pick one to work on. So I picked isolation. Um . . . I'm pretty independent. But I learned from Pastor Muren that men need other men, and I wanted to work on that. So I started a small group called Brothers in Arms. It was me and Jake and Wally and Isaac."

Wait. Wally got to be in Gabe's man club, but not me? I was ten times the man Wally was. The dude went into a panic attack whenever he touched dirt.

"I also started a band this year," Gabe said. "The small group is all like-minded guys who can hold each other accountable. But the band was just for fun. I thought it was important to spend time with different kinds of guys, not just the ones who thought like me."

"And how is all that going?" Mr. S asked.

"Brothers in Arms sort of fell apart when Jake went to college. And I still need a bass player for the band." Gabe looked at me.

I chuckled. I was *not* playing in his band. "So I don't think like you?"

"No way," Gabe said, grinning.

Well, at least he was honest. And I didn't want to be in Brothers in Arms, anyway, so there.

"And that's okay," Mr. S said. "It's important to learn how to get along with all types of people, but also to be bold enough to speak the truth when we feel our brother needs to hear it."

Gabe had spoken the truth to me *way* too many times.

"Today we graduate Gabe into adulthood," Mr. S said. "But to do that, he must act out the five attributes of manhood that I taught him years ago."

And on and on it went. The attributes of manhood were to serve others; to fight for what was right; to be a provider; to be a steward of time, money, and body; and to be a leader.

Mr. S made Gabe do feats of manhood in front of us, like melt an ice cube in his fist and wash Pastor Muren's feet—which I thought was hysterical.

And what did feet washing have to do with being a man, anyway?

Then Mr. S gave Gabe a purity ring, which he swore to wear as a sign of his commitment to his future wife. He said his household would serve and worship God with integrity and loyalty.

For some reason, the way Gabe said all that, the tone he used, it gave me a chill. It was like he knew he'd have a family and already knew how things would roll in his place.

The idea of me having my own family someday had never once crossed my mind.

And so Gabe put the ring on the ring finger of his right hand and showed it to everyone, beaming like a kid on Christmas morning. It was fat and shiny silver, with black writing that said, "Man of God" on one side and "True love waits" on the other.

It was kind of cool. Not that I wanted one or anything.

Then Mr. S went all Food Network and gave Gabe a paper sack. He had to go cook lunch for everyone using everything in the sack. The rest of us went outside where Mr. S had set up all kinds of competitions.

There was wood chopping, target shooting with BB guns, darts, horseshoes, canoeing across the lake, and archery—that one looked so easy when Legolas did it in the movies, but trust me, it wasn't.

After the contests we all went back into the cabin and found the tables set with paper plates and plastic forks. Gabe served up some kind of vegetable pasta with a white sauce that was a little runny but tasted good. There was also peas, garlicky toast, and butterscotch pudding for desert.

"There was a lot of milk and cream in that bag," Gabe said, when he finally joined us to eat.

"I wouldn't have a clue how to make Alfredo sauce from scratch," Lukas said.

"I wouldn't have a clue how to make if from a jar," I said.

But I was joking. I could heat a jar of sauce in the microwave, though I wasn't sure how to cook noodles.

When we'd all eaten, Mr. S had one final feat of manhood for Gabe. He had to answer the questions of those younger than him, which meant Lukas, Wally, and me.

"What is the meaning of life?" I asked.

A couple people chuckled, including Lukas.

But Gabe said, "To 'love the Lord your God with all your heart and with all your soul and with all your mind.' And to 'love your neighbor as yourself.' "

Oh-kay. Didn't see that coming.

Wally asked most of the questions. He started out okay with questions like, "What is the purpose of all this manhood stuff?" and "Why does a guy need a manhood party?" But then his questions got weird like, "Do you think crying is a sign of weakness?" and "What's your philosophy on homeschooling versus private Christian school versus public school?"

Gabe kept up with him, though, answering each one like the well-trained Boy Scout he was.

I wanted to ask something about sex, just because it would have been funny to make Gabe answer in front of his dad. But I wimped out.

"Do you consider cooking and cleaning a woman's work?" Lukas asked.

"Nice one," I said, giving Lukas a nod of approval.

"No," Gabe said. "In a marriage, if that's what you mean, I think that stuff should be a team effort, unless my wife chose not to work and had more time. I guess it's just something we'd figure out as a team. A wife is not a husband's maid."

Then Lukas started asking sex questions, the gutsy punk. But he didn't do it the way I'd wanted to. To embarrass Gabe.

He was being serious.

And Gabe answered seriously too.

And Lukas kept asking.

Talk about a Bermuda Triangle moment.

"I get that guys shouldn't pressure a girl to have sex," Lukas said. "But what's so bad about casual sex if the girl wants to? If it's her idea?"

I looked back to Gabe. Yeah, Mr. Boy Scout. What about that?

"It doesn't matter if the girl wants to," Gabe said. "The Bible is clear that sexual immorality is wrong. And sex was never meant to be casual. In fact, casual sex is a lie that leaves nothing but regret. It's two people using each other's bodies. And God says our bodies are his temple. We're not animals, you know. We *can* be self-controlled. It's possible."

"So I'd have to tell her no?" Lukas asked, as if Gabe was borderline psychotic for even suggesting it.

"Why not? A man can say no. He should. He should be the strong one, the responsible one. He should strive to protect any girl he meets and never look at her like she's a target."

Target. Gee . . . where had I heard *that* before, Mr. S?

"Spencer?"

I jumped. Mr. S was staring at me. "What?"

"There must be something you could ask Gabe."

"Uh . . ." I'd asked that meaning of life question. And I couldn't think of anything else. Not even a joke. My brain was on manhood overload. "I'm going to take a rain check," I said. "I need time to think of the perfect question."

"Okay, I like that," Mr. S said, surprising me. "Gabe is leaving this place an adult. And as his friend, Spencer, you can always go to him with questions. And he can go to you."

41

Sure. Like Gabe would ever ask my advice on anything.

After the Q&A, Mr. S prayed a big formal blessing over Gabe's life, then gave him a copy of the prayer, framed. Odd. Then Mr. S asked us all to share stories about Gabe. That part was pretty fun, actually. It went on for about an hour. When we ran out of stories, Mr. S gave Gabe the floor, and he thanked everyone and said he felt ready to take on the world, no matter what tough decisions he might have to face. After that we all gathered around Gabe, and the old dudes prayed out loud.

And then we were back in Jake's truck, headed to LA.

"So what'd you think?" Jake asked.

"A little archaic," I said, "and I'm still trying to imagine any scenario where I would tell a girl no."

Jake chuckled at that.

But Lukas said, "Arianna Sloan."

"Eww. Okay, you got me," I said.

"Hey!" Jake glared at me, then at Lukas in his rearview mirror. "Don't be mean."

"Sorry," Lukas said. "I mean, it was cool and all, how all those guys came out to support Gabe. But my dad would never do anything like that. I mean, we talk and stuff and it's good. But, I don't know, our culture is different, I guess."

"How so?" Jake asked.

"In Cuba, we flirt. We romance. We enjoy each other. We got to practice winning the ladies, because when we find the one we want to marry, we have to win her. And maybe there's some other guy who wants her too. So I gotta be the best if I'm gonna win my woman's heart, you know?"

No, I didn't know anything. I'd never won any girl for more than a week, and then it hadn't even been my idea.

Lukas and Jake kept talking about Cuban and American culture, but I tuned them out. My mind was filled with phrases they'd talked about today: defending the weak, being a provider, striving for excellence, honoring your commitments, being self-controlled, remaining accountable for your actions, having integrity, being loyal. And then Gabe's three Rs: respectful, responsible, and righteous.

I liked the sound of all that. I mean, who didn't want to be a hero? I'd wear a Batman cape if I could, you know? But it just seemed way too hard. Impossible even.

Still, as weird as the whole day was, I was a little jealous that Gabe's dad had done all that for him, and for so many years. That he'd made such a big deal about him becoming a man.

I'd be seventeen at the end of February. If Gabe had become a man at fourteen, did that mean Mr. S thought I wasn't a kid anymore? And if I wasn't a kid, was anyone going to tell me I was a man? Or was I just supposed to start acting like one?

I didn't have a clue.

REPORT NUMBER: 4

REPORT TITLE: I Take a Road Trip with My Grandma
SUBMITTED BY: Agent-in-Training Spencer Garmond
LOCATION: I-10 Eastbound, Just Past Beaumont, California
DATE AND TIME: Sunday, January 1, 2:44 p.m.

GRANDMA AND I LEFT FOR ARIZONA after church on Sunday. The drive was looong! Since U of A was the real reason for this trip, we passed through Phoenix and headed for Tucson. We'd visit ASU on the way back, though they were just about last on my interest list.

U of A had a "White Out" game against Stanford on Monday, and Coach Pasternack, an assistant coach at Arizona, said that was the best day to come. He said I wouldn't get to talk to the head coach—Sean Miller—very much, but he'd get me a short meeting.

When we got to Tucson, I texted Coach Pasternack, and he told me to join him the next morning at 8:00 a.m. for a short meeting with Coach Miller. I didn't like having to meet the head coach before I even got a tour, but it was a game day, so I had to make the best of it.

Grandma and I stayed the night in a Super 8 Motel and

got up bright and early for my meeting. Though I'd done this before, it was my first time visiting one of the schools that had shown interest in me, and I was really nervous.

We met Coach Pasternack outside the McHale Center. He was with Arizona guard Jordin Mayes, who had a chin beard that reminded me of C-Rok's buddy Ant Trane.

"Morning, Spencer," Coach Pasternack said, shaking my hand. "And you must be Alice Garmond." He shook Grandma's hand next. "Call me Coach P."

Jordin stuck out his hand next. "Jordin Mayes. It's cool to meet you."

"Hey, yeah, you too." I shook his hand. I was maybe an inch taller, which, for some reason, made me feel better. I deserved to be here. I needed to calm down.

"We don't have a lot of time this morning," Coach P said, "so let's get you in so you can talk to Coach Miller as long as possible."

"Do you need my profile and transcripts?" I asked.

"Nope, your coach sent those in. And I gave them to Coach Miller last night, so he will have already reviewed them."

Coach P led us through the McHale Memorial Center, giving us a bit of a tour as we went. "We'll show you the locker rooms on the way out."

"So you play point guard?" Jordin asked me.

"Yeah, but I'm a combo guard. You like it here?"

"Oh yeah. This is a great school. And the team is a family. We're all really close."

Yeah, that's what they all said. I wondered if it were actually true anywhere and how I'd be able to tell.

We went straight to Coach Miller's office. My heart felt like it had climbed down into my stomach and started a war. I wanted to impress these guys, but at the moment, I was too nervous to speak.

Before I knew it, Grandma Alice and I were shaking Coach Miller's hand. Coach P and Jordin said they'd wait outside, so it was just the three of us.

"I'm sorry I don't have much time today, Spencer," Coach Miller said. "Thanks for meeting with me so early."

"Yeah, no problem."

"Were you able to see the campus yesterday?"

"No, we got in late," Grandma said.

"We're going to check it out today," I added. "Before the game."

"It should be a good game. You looking into Stanford too? In fact, why don't you tell me who else you're talking to."

I took a deep breath and tried to remember what my coach had told me to say. "Uh, right now there's a lot of interest, and I'm trying to figure out how real it all is, you know? I've talked to coaches at UCLA, California, Stanford, and Arizona State. Uh, my coach has also talked to Gonzaga and New Mexico, but I haven't talked to them yet."

"Is that your interest, the way you listed those teams?"

I thought it over. "For the most part, yeah."

"And where do we fit in?"

Everyone said to be honest. "Second, I guess? I'm a big fan of UCLA, so I'd like to go there, but I also really like Arizona. You and UCLA are my top two. I'm, uh, curious about Gonzaga, but it's a long way from home. If they don't bring me up there, I'll probably take them off my list. I'd really like to play for the Pac 12." I said all that way too fast.

"You visit UCLA?"

"Yeah, I did."

"But no offers?"

"No, sir." Not yet.

He smiled. "You got any questions for me?"

"Some, yeah." I opened my notebook where I'd scribbled down my questions for Arizona. Coach had taught me all the things I should ask, but I'd added a few questions of my own. The first one seemed gutsy, but what did I have to lose? "How come you don't play Gabe York more? He was in the top twenty recruits in the country last year."

"It's nothing on Gabe; he's a great player. We just had a stock of veteran guards. Now is too early to talk starters for next season, but I'm sure things will change some."

I didn't know what to think about that. It was something that had nagged in the back of my mind. I didn't want to come to a school and sit on the bench. It wasn't realistic that I'd start as a freshman, but I'd like to at least make second string.

"We recruit experienced players at U of A," Coach Miller said. "Everyone can score, our bench is deep, we dominate on defense, we have stars in every position. We're looking to win a championship here, and we recruit champions."

Nice speech. "Okay. So, where do I stand in the recruiting class?"

"I won't lie to you. We're looking at a lot of guys, but we've liked what we've seen from you so far. We're not ready to offer you, but I'd sign you right now as a walk on. Maybe that will change as I see you play your senior year, though."

Walk on? That was no good. *Focus, Spencer.* "Uh, okay, so what do you think I should work on to improve?"

"From what I've seen of you, I'd like to see you consistently perform on the defensive end and in rebounding."

"Okay." But really? That seemed like a generic answer.

Had Coach Miller even watched my highlight video? I knew there was rebounding footage on there. I was one of the best rebounders on my team.

"How come you don't play AAU?" Coach Miller asked.

I shrugged. "Never knew much about it. I grew up playing street ball. Then my grandma put me in Pilot Point Christian, and I've been tight with my coach. He has his summer program. But I'm thinking about getting on a team this season."

"I'd really like to see that. I've only got another minute or so. Any other questions?"

Man, that went fast. I looked at my list. There were other questions, sure, but none of them seemed to matter much, knowing he was only offering me a walk-on spot.

"What about a scholarship?" Grandma Alice said.

Ug. I needed to teach her a little more about all this. "Walk-on means no scholarship, Grandma."

"No scholarship *at first*," Coach Miller said. "But if you come play for us, we'll do what we can to change that."

"Why can't you give him one now?" Grandma asked. "He's a very good player."

My face filled with heat. "Grandma . . ."

"It's a good question," Coach Miller said. "We only have so many scholarships for the team, Mrs. Garmond. And right now we've either passed those out to other players or offered them to prospects." He stood and walked around his desk.

I stood too, guessing we were done. "Thanks for your time," I said, feeling like an idiot and not too sure why.

Coach Miller shook my hand. "My pleasure, Spencer. I hope we get to talk more this summer and fall. Game days are not the best for visits, but I understand you've got to come when you can. And I do appreciate your making the drive."

And that was that. Coach P and Jordin gave us a tour of the locker rooms, which were *amazing*, and showed us the court, which was *beautiful*. I also got to see the room filled with Nike shoes. Each player got three pairs of shoes at the start of the season. I also saw the weight room, the second gym, the conditioning facility, and the trophy case.

It was all psychotically sweet.

Coach P and Jordin passed us off to a guy named Greg who gave us the rest of the campus tour since Coach P and Jordin had to get ready for the game.

"If you were here on any other day, Jordin would have taken you everywhere," Greg, who was a sports management major, said. "You could have even stayed the night in his dorm room."

"That would have been cool," I said.

The place was huge, and Grandma started slowing down. We left her at a coffee shop on campus while we went to look at the computer science building and the dorms. Greg told me which NBA players had come from U of A, including Luke Walton, Mike Bibby, and Jordan Hill. Then he went on for ten minutes about how Jerry Bruckheimer was also an alumni and what he thought of the *Pirates of the Caribbean* franchise.

"Athletes are treated really well here, especially basketball players since this is a basketball school," Greg said. Then he went on to tell me about the parties and the girls and all the cool extracurricular stuff that went on at U of A. "Think your old lady would let you come out with me later? Not much going on around here on a Monday night, but I could probably get something started."

I laughed at the very idea. "Nah, my grandma won't go for

that."

When we got back to Grandma, Greg still asked if he could take me out.

"Young man, this is a sixteen-year-old boy you are talking about here. I am not letting him out of my sight!"

"Told you," I said.

I loved what I saw of the place, though. And when Greg took us to the game, I was floored by the full arena, all dressed in white, screaming for their team. I wanted to play for a crowd like that. We had really good seats, and I could see Gabe York sitting on the bench. I wished I could ask him what he thought of the place. He had a Facebook page, so maybe I could connect there.

And then it was Tuesday morning, and we were driving back to Phoenix. It took us about an hour and forty minutes to get to the ASU college campus.

The recruiting coach from Arizona State was named Larry Greer. I texted him when we got close, and he sent a few students to meet us in front of the Wells Fargo Arena: freshman forward Eric Jacobsen, a pretty brown-haired girl named Lisa, and a transfer student named Max.

"This was a good day to come," Eric said. "There's not much going on, so we can spend all day with you."

Eric talked up the team as he led us to the locker rooms, then onto the court of the Arizona State University Sun Devils, where a bunch of players and the coaching staff were waiting. I instantly spotted point guard Jahii Carson and senior Carrick Felix, who was probably going to enter the draft this year.

Wow. No other school had taken this much effort.

"It's really great to meet you, Spencer," head coach Herb Sendek said. "We've been keeping track of you."

"Thanks," I said, feeling a little overwhelmed with everyone looking at me. "Nice to meet you too."

"You were at Arizona yesterday, that right?"

"Yes, sir."

"How did that go?"

"Uh, good. It was a game day, so they were busy."

"They offer you?"

I tried to look proud. "As a walk-on."

"*Walk-on?*" Eric said, as if the idea were ludicrous.

"It's still early," Coach Sendek said, "and you're not on the AAU circuit. Those AAU players are in coaches' heads more since we see them play in tournaments."

"I was thinking of joining an AAU team," I said. "Might be too late, though."

"Not if you got on a good team. And it would help you get seen by more coaches. But let me ask you, what's your goal?"

I loved no-brainer questions. "To play college ball where I'm a good fit for the team. I'd like to play point. I like orchestrating and feeding people the ball. I think that's my biggest strength."

"And what would you say is your biggest weakness?"

"Driving through the defense. I need to get a lot stronger if I'm going to go to the basket against some of these bigger guys." I gestured to Jordan Bachynski, who was seven foot two. "And I could be faster on my feet."

"What about turnovers?" one of the assistant coaches asked.

"I can steal the ball from anyone." I grinned, and some of the guys laughed.

"We can get you strong," Coach Sendek said. "We work hard to develop our players. Look at the success of some of our guys. James Harden, Jeff Pendergraph, Julius Hodge, Cedric Simmons, Wally Szczerbiak, Eric Murdock, Eric Boateng. All of these guys have had longtime NBA careers, and we helped them develop as players. ASU is where they got their start.

"We're also looking for guys with great character. Your coach told me a lot about you and how you've worked hard to stay out of trouble. I like that. And I like players who have your kind of passion for the game. But we ultimately want players who want to be here. That's important to us. We don't want to be anyone's last resort. The guys who want to be at Arizona State ultimately are going to be very successful."

And I had never wanted to come here. So maybe I should just say that. Instead I asked, "Why do you want me?"

"One of our responsibilities as coaches is to put our players in the best position to be successful," Coach Sendek said. "Talented and coach-able don't come along very often, but when they're paired, great things can happen. I've seen your game tapes. I've talked to your coach. You're a special kind of player, Spencer. With your competitive toughness and high basketball IQ, I see you have two options. You could go mid-major and they'll want you to score. Or you could play for the Pac 12 and orchestrate and be a floor general. Your primary goal would be to get the athletes the ball. That's what we'd like to see from you at ASU. And we're extending you an offer to come play for us that includes a full scholarship."

Really? "Wow. Thanks." It sounded exactly like what I wanted in a team, but I'd never wanted ASU, so I didn't know what to say. I remembered what the NCSA resource guide said to say when you get an offer and parroted it back. "It's still early for me. I'd like to talk about it with my grandma and my coach. Plus I'd kind of like to see if I'll go on any official visits.

How long does your offer stand?"

"We're looking at some other guys too, but I think it's safe to say you have until the end of September before a lot of decisions start being made. If you have any questions, don't hesitate to call."

We talked a while longer, but it started to seem like Coach Sendek was repeating himself, so I complimented their facilities, which got some of the guys to give me another tour of the locker rooms and weight rooms and stuff.

Jahii came with me this time, so I asked him what he liked about playing for ASU.

"Our guys are tough," Jahii said. "They can run up and down the court with me, and it's great feeding them the basketball, knowing they're going to be able to finish. It's a point guard's dream, man. And these guys are fun to be around too. I love playing with them."

"I wish I could play with you guys, but that's against the rules," I said.

"It's against the rules to play here, but we can go over to the rec center and shoot around."

I didn't know if that was true or not, but I figured, who would know?

So after our tour and after we said goodbye to the coaches, Jahii, Eric, Lisa, Max, and Jordan Bachynski headed over the rec center to shoot around. Grandma sat on the bleachers and watched as Eric, Jordan, and I played three on three against Jahii, Lisa, and Max. Lisa turned out to be on the women's college team and was a good shot. Max sucked, so Jahii and Lisa did all the work. And I had fun playing with a guy almost a full foot taller than me.

• • •

I went home a lot confused. I'd been so certain that, out of my choices, I wanted to play for Arizona. But I wasn't sure I wanted to walk on, not that I could even afford to. Grandma didn't have the money to pay my way through college, so the scholarship offer was a big deal. And I certainly didn't want to play where I wasn't needed. Arizona could get anyone, but ASU wanted me and that felt good.

I went to Kip's house on Friday before our game and filled him in on the trip. He logged onto his computer, told me there was something I had to see.

"ASU sucked up because they need you more," Kip said.

"They don't *need* me. They've got Jahii." And Jahii was an incredible point guard.

"Yeah, but he'll go to the NBA before he graduates. They'll want to make sure they have another floor general."

"Maybe." And if so, that would be a great opportunity to get lots of playing time.

"Okay, dude, check it. It's a frat party at University of Arizona."

"That one that was all over the news for the fight?"

"That was ASU. Just watch."

So I did. It was a bunch of guys going to buy two cartloads of alcohol at some store, then they were sitting around tables outside at night, talking. Then the party started. Dancing girls. Guys smashing full beer cans open on their foreheads. Two girls making out. Some guy drinking a beer underwater in the pool. Lots of grinding on the dance floor. Lots of kissing. Then a siren. Bottles and trash floating in the pool the next morning.

"You could go here." Kip dragged the slider back. The

video started again, and Kip paused it on a girl who was dancing in her underwear. "You could dance with that girl."

"I'm not joining a fraternity," I said. "Besides, I really liked what Coach Sendek had to say."

"Coaches say that stuff on purpose, man. They're trying to sign you."

"Well, Coach Miller didn't say anything like that. I'm not sure he'd even watched my game tapes."

"Arizona is in the running, though. ASU, not so much."

"*I know*. But ASU is offering me the better deal."

"But not better parties," Kip sang. "At least not on YouTube."

"I'm not picking a school based on their YouTube parties. There are parties everywhere."

"Including my Jolt Revolt on March 3."

This ticked me off. "Why couldn't you have waited until after state?"

"Because it had to be in before March 15 to count for the freebies. Calm yourself, you prude. We're not going to get in trouble."

We'd better not. I had *way* too much on the line.

REPORT NUMBER: 5

REPORT TITLE: I Fall Off a Mountain and Almost Die
SUBMITTED BY: Agent-in-Training Spencer Garmond
LOCATION: Pilot Point Mountain, Pilot Point, California
DATE AND TIME: Saturday, January 7, 9:06 a.m.

THE FIRST SATURDAY IN JANUARY, the Mission League met in the Verdugo Mountains for our first OST hike. The land around us was covered in sagebrush, dirt, and rocks since it never snowed and rarely rained.

The first thing I noticed? Grace wasn't there. But school didn't start back up until next Wednesday, so maybe she and her family were still in Miami.

"Today we're doing a casualty evacuation," Mr. S said. "One of your team was hurt in a fall. He's drifting in and out of consciousness. You use your cell phone to call for help, but the terrain is too difficult for a rescue helicopter to land, and it can't get close enough to send down a winch because of strong wind gusts."

"I don't feel any wind," I murmured to Gabe.

"Your team must move your injured man down the mountain to the evacuation spot, which I've marked with an orange flag. You have no stretcher, but you do have some walking sticks, a climbing rope, a tent, and the gear in your packs. It's a race, but you need to be careful. I'll be watching to see how you treat your injured man. Extra points for correct first aid."

"Who's the injured person?" Arianna asked.

"Your biggest teammate is injured," Mr. S said.

Great. I was the biggest person in our whole school, height wise. Wally was pudgy, but not pudgy enough to outweigh me.

"I weight 152," Wally said, as if it weren't completely obvious which one of us was the biggest.

"155," Gabe said, though he had three inches on Wally. "How about you, Spencer?"

I'd put on twenty pounds of muscle since last summer with all my workouts and a high protein diet. Plus I'd gained an inch and a half in height. "182."

"Man!" Gabe said.

"I can't help being awesome," I said.

Nick was the biggest on Diakonos team. He was about Gabe's size. Diakonos had their whole team while we were missing Grace. But I guess she wouldn't have been much help carrying me, anyway.

Mr. S took the Diakonos team to another spot where he could time them, and we couldn't see what each other was doing. Kerri stayed to time us. She made me lay down in the dirt.

"Okay," she said after getting a text. "You can start now."

"Give me the tent," Gabe said.

"We're supposed to do first aid," Wally said.

"Right." Gabe crouched down at my side.

I made a gagging noise. "Can't . . . breathe . . ."

"Where does it hurt?" Gabe asked me.

"Actually, I think I can get up and walk," I said. "That will get us there first for sure."

"*Spencer*," Kerri warned.

"Okay, fine. My neck hurts, and I think I broke my ankle."

"What will the recruiting coaches say?" Gabe asked.

"Ha ha." So not funny to even think about that.

"Okay," Gabe said. "So let's put something under his neck, then figure out how to use this stuff to make a stretcher."

"Many people mistake ankle fractures for sprains," Wally said, "but they're quite different injuries."

Gabe pulled a T-shirt out of his pack and started rolling it. "We don't have to make a diagnosis. And if he's on a stretcher, I'm not worried about his ankle." Gabe crouched beside me and tucked the T-shirt under my neck.

"But we can't move him if his neck might be broken," Wally said. "We'd be wiser to ask the helicopter to land and have their men come up here with a stretcher."

"That's not the assignment," I said. "Stop arguing and listen to Gabe."

"We can use my notebook to stabilize his head and shoulders when we pick him up," Gabe said.

Wally sighed. "Fine."

So I stayed on the ground while Gabe and Wally argued over how to attach the tent flysheet to the walking sticks. First they tied one side's ties to the other, but when they stuck the sticks through, it was way too wide, even for me. My rear end would have been dragging on the ground. Next, they folded it in half but couldn't figure out how to attach it to the sticks.

"What if you just wrapped the climbing rope around it as much as you could, then draped the flysheet over it to make a cot?" I suggested.

So they tried it. But the rope wasn't long enough and only went around the sticks four times, hardly enough to support me.

"Forget the flysheet," Gabe said. Let's just use our jackets."

"How?" Wally asked.

Gabe took his off, zipped it up, and tucked in the sleeves. Then he threaded the poles in the sleeve holes and back out the waist.

"Nice, Gabe," I said.

Wally removed his coat slowly. "I didn't put on sunscreen this morning."

Gabe snatched Wally's coat from him and got it threaded up the end of the sticks. "We really need three coats if we're going to support his legs too."

"I got a spare T-shirt in my bag," I said.

Gabe found my shirt and put it on the end of the sticks. He laid the stretcher beside me on the ground and pulled the sticks as far apart as they'd go. "Okay, Wally, you get his feet. On the count of three we lift him. Not very high. Just straight to the stretcher."

I couldn't believe they actually got me on the thing. Gabe put his notebook under my head. It felt too small to support anything. They started carrying me up the incline, but I slid backwards and had to grab the covered walking sticks to keep from sliding right off the end.

"Guys, hey!"

"Wally, catch up to me," Gabe said. "We'll go sideways up the hill."

Once Wally caught up, they sidestepped their way to the top. The sky was bright and covered in fluffy clouds. It was kind of fun to let them cart me around.

By the time they got to the main trail and started taking the switchbacks down the mountain, I could see Lukas, Isabel, and Arianna coming down a different switchback. They had Nick on their tent's flysheet. It looked like they'd rolled the walking sticks up from the edges of the tent until they had a nice stretcher. Smart. Probably Arianna's idea.

We barely beat them to the orange flag, but Mr. S gave them more points for first aid. Arianna had bandaged Nick's leg and put a neck brace on him.

"Seriously? Who packs a neck brace?" I said. "That's just nuts."

"It's never nuts to be prepared," Arianna said.

"I, for one, am thankful for my teammate's foresight," Nick said. "The way I see it, I recovered fully, but Garmond is paralyzed for life."

See? I knew Nick's kindness wouldn't last long.

• • •

Grace didn't show at church on Sunday either, and Arianna said she was supposed to have been back by now.

She didn't answer any of my texts or Facebook messages.

It was kind of freaking me out.

So I walked over to Ghetoside—a Pilot Point nickname for the Meadowside Apartments where Grace lived. Her place was on the ground floor and faced the street. The driveway in front was empty. The lights were off. I even knocked on the door, but no one was home.

I let it go for a few days, but when school started and Jaz said Grace hadn't been in class, I started going by her place more often.

And one night, the lights were on, and an old Honda Civic was parked in the driveway. I went and knocked on the door. I could hear the TV all the way out here, but I guessed the walls weren't very thick. I should probably question the neighbors. See if they'd heard anything from the place. I could ask Kip's dad if there had been any calls to the cops for this address.

The front door jerked open. A man stood there holding a can of Budweiser. He was wearing worn jeans and a T-shirt with Kurt Busch's race car on it. He had buzz-cut blond hair and the reddish skin that usually came with heavy drinking—something Mr. S had taught us. He also reeked like a kegger.

"Mr. Thomas?" I asked.

"Who wants to know?"

Oh, yeah. He was *so* cool. "I'm Spencer Garmond. One of Grace's friends. We both went to Okinawa last summer."

"She's not here. She's in Miami with her mom."

"But I thought that was just for Christmas."

"They didn't come back. I think they're staying there."

His indifference ticked me off. "Maybe it's because you beat them up," I said. "Or maybe Grace isn't in Miami at all because you hurt her too bad this time."

"Listen here, you cocky little . . ." And I left out the rest of what he called me since this is an official report and all. But he basically told me to get off his property or he'd call the cops.

So I left.

And I *really* hoped I hadn't made things worse for Grace.

•   •   •

January breezed by. The same schools were still talking to

coach about me, except Berkley had offered early, which made no sense to me until Coach said he'd told them I wanted to study computers and work for the CIA.

So, Grandma and I went north to visit Berkley and Stanford—two schools I'd never get into on academics alone. We even got to watch them play each other at Stanford, which won by ten. Stanford played better than they had when I watched them against the Arizona Wildcats. I definitely liked them better than Berkley, which was kind of a tree hugging school. But UC Berkley had a campus attaché for the CIA. If the NBA and the Mission League didn't pan out, maybe I could still be a spy—with a gun, even.

I ranked my choices based on who'd shown interest: Arizona State, Arizona Wildcats, Stanford, Berkley. And then there was Gonzaga. A great team. Good coaching staff from what I could tell. Far away, though. Not a power school or a power conference.

At this point, I wasn't going to choose early. I'd wait until the fall and see if anyone would bring me in for an official visit. Hopefully by then UCLA would have a chance to see more of me.

The League continued to have Saturday OST days. We drove up to Big Bear and did a day of snow survival, went rock climbing at Miniholland in the Santa Monica Mountains, and started one-Saturday-a-month scuba diving classes down in Venice where this tattooed chick, Blaire, had mercy on me and taught me to tread water and do that crawl-stroke breathing thing—my crawl stroke still sucked.

Still no Grace, but she did text back to say she was staying in Miami a while longer. I asked her to text me what she'd written on my back in Okinawa as a code phrase, just to make sure it wasn't her dad trying to get rid of me. But she answered correctly.

And then it was February. Our team was 21-2. Playoffs were coming, and we were in great shape to win the section finals and make state.

Everything was on track. I just had to keep on swimming.

•   •   •

The first Saturday in February found the League up in Topanga Canyon Park for a day of concealment training, which was basically playing hide and seek. Alpha team would go first, and Diakonos would be timed on how fast they could find us. After lunch, we'd switch. I remembered from our last trip up here that there was no cell service, so I'd worn my grandpa's wristwatch. I hated not knowing the time.

We stood in the parking lot by the open back door of Mr. S's minivan where he had bins of camo clothing, nets with leaves, and military face paints.

"The purpose of camouflage is to hide yourself and your equipment from the enemy," he said.

"Camouflage predates humanity, Mr. Stopplecamp," Wally said. "It started when our Creator designed animals to naturally adapt and blend in with their environment."

"Thank you for that, Wally," Mr. S said. "For us humans, however, two elements help concealment: color and pattern. Colors match your surroundings and patterns conceal the contours of your hidden shape. When we see things, our perception recognizes certain objects. If we're looking for a spruce tree, we look for a long, brown trunk and dark green branches. But if that tree was painted like camouflage it would be much harder to see."

I knew this already. We'd done a bunch of camouflage experiments last fall, including creating hidden patterns and shapes out of Legos and painting rubber balls with camo paint.

Today we were going to paint each other.

And still no Grace. Major frown. I was glad that she was safe and sound in Miami, but I kind of missed her snark. And the smell of coconuts.

To make things fair, since the teams were uneven, Alpha team also got to hide a duffle bag, which we agreed was about the size of Grace. That way each team had to make four finds.

The morning was overcast and foggy, which gave us an advantage in hiding first since the fog would burn off by lunch time. But Diakonos could learn from our mistakes, which might help them hide better when their turn came.

Kerri waited at the van with Diakonos, and Mr. S helped Gabe, Wally, and me carry the bags of gear up to the public restrooms, which reeked, by the way.

"You guys have a half hour to get yourselves ready and hide," Mr. S said. "Don't waste it."

We pulled out two tan and brown camo outfits, and two green and brown ones.

I'll tell you what—a half hour is not long enough for three guys to get themselves dressed in camouflage when one of those guys is Wally. We all got dressed fine—Gabe and Wally in the greens and me in the tan, since it was the only thing that would fit—but when I tried to rub green paint on Wally's face, he started hyperventilating. Gabe attempted to reason with him, but we eventually gave up and made him wear a dark green and brown camo net over his clothing. By the time we were ready, we only had seven minutes to hide.

"Let's split up," I said. "You and Wally find a place in the woods. I'll go up to the rocky areas with the duffle." Which I had wrapped in the other tan camo shirt.

And so we ran for it. Gabe and Wally ditched me in the woods, and I kept going up. I was in excellent shape, and it was early and still cool, but by the time I ran halfway to Eagle Rock, I really wanted to peel off some layers.

The fog was awesome. The higher I got, the less I could see. It was like walking inside a cloud. I probably was.

It occurred to me that I'd picked the wrong clothing. There was a lot more greenery up here than I remembered from our last hike, and the duffle and I were dressed to blend in with rock and dirt. I kept my eye out for rockier ground. If it came down to it, I could probably hide in one of the caves up top, but Diakonos would instantly find me if one of them looked inside.

I passed a cluster of small boulders. The biggest one was the size of a yoga ball, the smallest the size of a basketball. I stashed the bag vertically behind some of the rocks and adjusted the shirt so it was smooth on the round end of the bag. That way it looked like one more boulder in the bunch. It almost seemed too easy.

But I still had my giant self to hide, and the time was up. Diakonos was probably already on its way.

I reached the top of Eagle Rock. Last time I stood there I'd been able to see the Santa Monica pier. Today I couldn't see ten feet in front of me. I looked down. It was a pretty straight drop. People like to rock climb here. Maybe if I went back a bit, where the bushes turned to rock . . .

I backtracked and found a steep incline, maybe twenty degrees. There were a couple decent footholds down there. Perhaps I could just stand, pressed against the rock.

It took me a while to get down. I wasn't the nimblest of climbers and ended up sliding most of the way. I had no idea how I was going to get back up. By the time I was in position, facing the cliff, my grandpa's watch read 10:37 a.m.

After running all that way wearing several layers and a hat and gloves, then standing in a precarious location for a half hour, I was burning up. I needed to get some air flowing before I passed out. So I unbuttoned the front of my jacket and untucked my T-shirt. The cool air snaked up my torso and into my pits and felt so nice.

Until it started to rain.

It wasn't a heavy rain, just a sprinkle, but it was enough to make me uncomfortable. Looking back, the whole thing was dumb and dumber. I didn't have any climbing gear to anchor myself. And Mr. S had spent all year preaching about being prepared for any weather conditions, which I was currently not.

"Man, I don't think he's up here."

My whole body tensed at the nearness of Lukas's voice.

"Yes, he is," Nick said. "Trust me. Garmond is used to looking down on the world."

"He's too big to be up here. We'd see him."

"Hey, Garmond!" Nick yelled. "You win! Come on out."

"That's cheating," Lukas said.

"There's no cheating in real life, Rodriquez," Nick said. "You survive, or you don't. If Garmond is dumb enough to fall for me yelling 'game over,' then we win. End of story."

"Whatever. I'm going to check the caves," Lukas said.

Good thing I hadn't hid in the caves.

"Hey, Lukas! Check out these trampled bushes!" Nick yelled, then mumbled, "Never mind."

Nick's steps magnified through the rock. It sounded like he was climbing above my head. I didn't dare move. A pebble fell down inches from my face, then a stone about the size of an Oreo. Then one hit the top of my head. I flinched.

"How the heck did you get down there, Garmond?"

Mother pus bucket. Of all the people who could have found me, why Nick?

I decided to stay put, hoping he wasn't positive he'd found me, that he was only guessing.

"Lukas! I found him! Mark the time!"

So much for that plan.

The sound of Lukas's footsteps grew as he ran my way. They suddenly stopped. "Wow!" he said. "How'd you get down there, man?"

I finally looked up, squinting against the rain sprinkling my face. "I slid."

Lukas chucked. "Now how you going to get back up?"

"Hadn't thought that far ahead."

"I say we leave him," Nick said.

Lukas got down on his stomach and reached out his hand. "Just grab on. We'll pull you up." He slapped Nick's leg. "Come on, man."

Nick groaned, but got down on his stomach as well. Yet I wasn't close enough to reach either of their hands. I needed a boost. I grabbed at the rock, looking for a handhold, but it was smooth. Gravity had gotten me down here, and it wasn't going to help me back up.

I looked down to see where I could get a foothold, and my shirt billowed in the way. Nice.

I lifted my foot, using the toe of my boot to feel for the foothold I knew was there. I should just tuck in my shirt so I could see the thing, but then my boot found it.

"Coming up." I jumped off the foothold. Lukas grabbed one of my hands, Nick the other, and they held me there, our bent arms straining.

Nick swore. "You weigh a ton, Garmond."

My boots pedaled against the rock, looking for another ledge. I felt my left hand slip a bit. "*Lukas.*"

"Our gloves are wet, man," Lukas said. "Go back down so we can get a better hold."

I gritted my teeth and breathed out my nose. "I can't go back down. I can't see the ledge."

"Try, man! Please! I'm dropping—" Lukas cursed.

My left hand slid from his. He fell back. Out of sight. My weight pulled Nick's arm straight, and I dropped several inches.

Nick reached his other hand over the ledge, trying to grab me with both. His body slid toward the edge. He reached his other hand back to anchor himself. "I'm going to drop him. Lukas!"

Lukas looked over the ledge again. "What can I do?"

"Hold me," Nick said. "He's slipping. I need both hands."

Lukas disappeared, and, I figured, grabbed onto Nick, who made a grab for me with his other hand.

But it was too late.

My glove slipped out of his and I fell.

I scraped down the rocky incline, going faster than I wanted to. My adrenaline skyrocketed. I fell through the top of a tree that was growing out of a crack in the rock. The branches clawed at me like some kind of werewolf. My face, hands, and chest got the worst of it. I floundered, grabbed a spindly top branch, but my fist slid right down it, popping off all the leaves and heating my palm through my glove.

And then I fell straight, off the cliff and down, like stepping off a diving board. Only there was no water to greet me. Only sagebrush, dirt, and rocks.

I was going to die.

But no. I could land it, maybe. Like jumping off the roof of a house.

I bent my knees, hoping to absorb my weight. I stuck the landing at first, but my torso shifted, twisting me. My left leg popped. I fell, hit the ground on my back, and kept sliding down the incline backwards, head first.

Mother pus bucket! My leg throbbed like I'd been electrocuted from hip to toe. I crossed my arms and tucked my chin against my chest like we learned until I slid to a stop in some chaparral.

I was shaking all over, hot, and focused entirely on the excruciating pain in my left leg. Or maybe it was my knee. Had I broken something? Oh God, please no.

I lifted my head and peered down at my leg. It looked okay. I didn't see any protruding bone. My T-shirt was torn and bloody. My chest stung. No, it was throbbing. Not as bad as my leg, but those branches had sliced through my shirt like Wolverine's claws.

I let my head fall back and looked up the rock face. I couldn't see Nick or Lukas. I couldn't even see Eagle Rock through the fog. Hopefully the guys had gone for help.

"Help," I said to myself.

My knee was throbbing. I could tell it was my knee now. I couldn't bend it. Trying to move my left leg sent fire up and down my whole side. I thought about trying to stand, but I couldn't even manage to push myself to sitting. It hurt too bad.

Oh, the game! Tonight. Basketball. We had three games left before the Southern Section playoffs. Tonight should be an easy win. But next week we had Oaks Christian, and they were tough. Had I just ended my team's chance at winning the playoffs? At winning state? My own career? The mere thought filled my eyes with hot tears.

No. Please no. Please, God?

I lay there in shock. Not quite the same kind of shock I'd experienced in Okinawa when Anya had cut me, but the shock of being here at all, of wondering what I'd just done to my chances of being recruited to play ball. Dizzying.

I replayed every mistake I'd made. Climbing down that incline without gear, unbuttoning my shirt, trying to jump up with no foothold and a bad grip.

Stupid. So stupid.

I heard people calling my name. I should probably answer, but all I could do was lie there, staring at the foggy sky, scared out of my mind.

Even after all our invent-a-stretcher training, Mr. S wouldn't move me. He had a CB radio and used it to call Kerri back at the van. She drove to within cell phone range and called 911.

Twenty minutes later Mr. S and I were airlifted to the Ronald Regan UCLA Medical Center, which, ironically, was only five blocks and a football field from the Pauley Pavilion where the Bruins played basketball.

This was the worst day of my life.

They gave me something for the pain, and I was gone.

• • •

I woke up in a hospital bed wearing a blue paper gown, feeling groggy. My left leg was in a fat brace. What did *that* mean? Wouldn't it be in a cast if it were broken?

"Look who's up." Grandma's voice.

I turned my head and found her sitting in the chair beside my bed. "What's wrong with my leg?"

"They did some tests, an MRI, and something to do with a scope. The doctor says you tore your ACL."

"What! No, no." I tried to sit up and my chest throbbed, felt stiff and wrong. I fell back to my pillow and caught my breath. "But torn ACLs . . . they only happen on the court or the field or the, the . . ."

"You also got twenty stitches on your face and chest combined."

Stitches? I didn't care about any stinking stitches. My hands were trembling. My chest was tight. Tears flooded my eyes. I tried and failed to fight them.

It was over. Everything. Done. Bye-bye, basketball.

I whispered a colorful stream of words that hadn't come out of my mouth in a year and a half.

"Spencer Michael Garmond, there is no cause to use that kind of language."

Oh, but there is, Grandma, I wanted to say. Instead I just stared at the ceiling and clamped my teeth together.

Grandma tried to cheer me up, but when I didn't respond to anything she said, she left on a mission to tell the doctor I was awake.

Who cared.

I lay there, hating everything. I felt claustrophobic. I wanted to get up, walk, at least roll on my side.

I tried, but whatever had happened to my chest wasn't

happy about me moving. I lifted the neckline of my paper dress and peered down . . .

And just about passed out.

Not because of the jagged black stitches down the front of my chest that made me look like something Dr. Victor Frankenstein had put back together. That was freaky, yes, but not all that surprising after Grandma's warning.

But the stitches were vertical, and they passed over the horizontal scar I'd gotten in Japan when Anya cut me. If this new injury left a scar . . . Holy figs! I would have a cross on my chest, the very thing Anya had said was true about the profile match. *"One of the prophecies states that the profile match will bear the mark of his faith."* Except, back then that hadn't been true about me. And now? Uh . . .

Before I could think more on that, the doctor came in with Grandma and blathered on about how I had a choice between surgery or straight physical therapy.

"Surgery," I said, swallowing another glob of tears that I'd managed to choke back. My emotions were out of whack. I wondered what was in my IV. "When can I get it?"

"Well, this isn't your hospital," the doc said. "You'll need to check with your insurance and set up an appointment."

"Can't you do it now?"

"No, it's not an emergency."

"But it is." It was. My team. My scholarship offers.

"Basketball means the world to Spencer, doctor," Grandma said. "He has some college scholarships to play for several different NCAA schools."

"Oh, I'm terribly sorry," the doctor said, which I guess . . . What else was he going to say? *Gee, let me get my magic wand and fix that up for you?* I'd been around long enough to know that a torn ACL was third only to paralysis and death in the world of sports. It was a minimum year out. A year that I'd lose playing for state with my team, playing on the AAU team, doing summer camp. A year of practice gone.

And there was no guarantee my knee would heal. No way of knowing that I'd be the same athlete.

When word got out, my offers were going to vanish.

REPORT NUMBER: 6

REPORT TITLE: I Have Dinner with a Movie Director
SUBMITTED BY: Agent-in-Training Spencer Garmond
LOCATION: I5 Northbound, Passing Through Echo Park,
California, USA
DATE AND TIME: Tuesday, February 7, 10:08 a.m.

I DIDN'T GO TO SCHOOL ON MONDAY. Grandma got me in to see my primary care physician so that he could refer me to a surgeon. On Tuesday, I skipped school again, and we went to St. Vincent Medical Center to consult with the surgeon. I didn't like all these appointments before I could get the surgery. I just wanted it done. And I wanted it done well.

I didn't like the surgeon at St. Vincent's, either. The nerdly Dr. Kapitankoff acted like he had more important things to do than help me. The whole time we were there, it was like he couldn't wait for us to leave.

"I think I should get a second opinion," I told Grandma on the ride home.

"What second opinion? Two doctors have confirmed it's a torn ACL."

"I don't doubt it's a torn ACL. I just don't think Dr.

Captain Crunch is the best guy for the job."

"You don't have a choice, young man. He's the only knee surgeon on our insurance."

Well, maybe our insurance wasn't good enough for me.

Many would say my basketball career was over because of the timing and nature of the injury. I wasn't convinced. I had the summer to recover, and I still had my senior year. That was plenty of time to get back in shape and prove myself.

So I was taking this surgery very seriously. I needed a surgeon who'd do the same. "Good enough" wasn't going to cut it. And Captain Crunch struck me as a "good enough" type of guy.

I wanted the guy Rajon Rondo had. Wonder how much he charged to fix a torn ACL? If only I knew a rich guy.

Then it hit me. I did. My dad.

The mere thought of contacting my dad left me a bit queasy, though that could have been Grandma's driving. I didn't dare bring up my idea for fear she'd say no.

Would he help me, though? Was it worth the risk to ask?

I've done a lot of dumb things for a lot of dumb reasons. But this was a dumb thing for a good reason. Right?

There was no one I could ask for advice. I was just going to have to decide. Arianna would likely say I should pray about it. I did have *the mark of my faith* scarred into my chest. That should count for something, right?

So I gave it a whirl.

I don't know how people like Arianna or Gabe heard answers to their prayers. I didn't hear anything. Just Grandma humming along to the "Sunshine on My Shoulders" song on her John Denver cassette.

Yes, cassette. Her Lincoln was *that* old.

And, no, the slow, sappy song did *not* make me happy. It was more like music to die by.

As we headed home, I played with my cell phone. Sue Adams, that reporter from the *Pilot Point Bulletin*, had called. Like I wanted to talk to her. And Coach Van Buren had called a few times. He must know I wasn't going to play in tomorrow's game. It was an away game, so at least there was no temptation for me to go watch and weep from the bench.

But I should call him. Tomorrow, maybe. I'd just go by his office tomorrow. Yeah.

Though I didn't know how I'd get there. Hobble down the sidewalk? I'd have to leave really early.

I suddenly wanted to scream.

Why was this happening to me? Why?

When we got home, it wasn't even lunchtime yet, so I told Grandma I was going to go lie down, then hop-jumped it to my room on the crutches the hospital had given me. Only I didn't lie down. Instead I got on Facebook, found the last message my dad had sent, and replied.

> Hey. I was wondering if we could talk. I need help
> and don't know who else to ask.
> Spencer

Now what? Kip was still in school. I clicked over to the UCLA Bruins basketball Facebook page. I'd barely made it through the first post when my dad replied with a phone number.

Okay then. I dialed him up.

He answered after one ring. "Spencer?"

"Yeah."

"Is this about your accident? I heard what happened."

My chest constricted. I was actually talking to my father. How did he know everything about me so quickly, anyway? "Uh, yeah. I need surgery."

"Your grandma doesn't have insurance?"

"No, she does. But . . . it's complicated. I need the best, and I'm not sure . . ."

"Say no more, Son. I can help. And I'd like to see you. Can I send a car to bring you to my place?"

Send a car? "Uh . . . I can get a ride down there. Can I bring a friend with me?"

"Sure, sure. I understand this is a bit awkward." His voice was calm and confident, like he was used to people asking him for favors. It wasn't what I'd expected.

Though I don't know what I'd expected. An apology, maybe?

He gave me his address, and we hung up. That was it.

Weird.

I was glad our team had early practice today. This was going to be tricky, and I needed Kip's—

A knock on the door. "Spencer?"

"Yeah?"

Grandma opened the door and peeked in. "I'm going to work. I left you a sandwich in the fridge. There are apples on the counter. Think you can get to the kitchen?"

"Yeah, I got it." Now was my chance. "Hey, Grandma? If Kip picks me up, can I go over to his house for a while?"

"For dinner?"

"Yeah, I guess." The longer she expected me gone, the better.

"You be careful with your leg. No playing basketball. And

be home by eight."

"Yes, ma'am. Thank you."

She grabbed my shoulder and kissed the top of my head, gave me her one-armed squeeze-hug. "It's going to be okay, you'll see."

I hoped she was right. I also hoped she'd understand if or when she found out what I'd done.

• • •

After practice, Kip came and picked me up in his Bimmer. When we got to his place, I asked him to park around the side of his house, hoping that Kimball and Mr. Sloan would park out front like they usually did.

"Why am I parking here?" Kip asked.

To make my plan happen, I had to tell Kip the truth. Some of it, anyway.

"Wait for it . . ." I held up a finger and watched in the rearview mirror as Kimbal's sedan neared. It passed by, then turned the corner. I pointed. "See that car? Those guys are following me."

Kip shot me a disbelieving smirk. "Is that a fact?"

"Yes. It is. Look, I'm not making this up, and I really need your help." I got out of the car and hopped on my good foot to the back door to retrieve my crutches. Easier said than done with my leg brace. Once I had them, I hop-jumped down the sidewalk.

Kip got out too. "Where are you going?"

"Front door. Watch and see."

Kip slammed his car door and followed. "You're a freak. You know that, right?"

I couldn't argue, not with the two scars forming a cross on my chest and the nightmares I kept having of Grace.

Kip caught up, and we followed the sidewalk to the corner and turned. Kimbal's sedan was just pulling up. As always, they'd turned around to get their favorite spot. Right across the street with a perfect view of the front door.

And no view of the back door.

I waved at Kimbal, then crutched up the walkway to Kip's front door.

"Who is that?" Kip asked, glancing back at the sedan.

"Kimbal."

"*Officer* Kimbal? I thought you were done having an SRO. What'd you do?"

"I didn't do anything. You want the truth? I'll tell you. But wait until we get inside."

"What's with the cloak and dagger—?"

"Dude. Please?"

Kip rolled his eyes. "Whatever, man."

Once we were inside, seated in the living room, and I was certain Kip's dad wasn't home, I was ready to spill a few beans. Not all of them, mind you, but enough to get Kip's help.

"You can't tell anyone," I said. "Not even Megan."

"Just spit it out, already."

I sighed and hoped I wasn't making a mistake. "Okay, so, my name is not Spencer Garmond. I'm in a witness protection thing and those guys are keeping me safe."

Kip blew a raspberry. "Since when?"

"Since I was two."

"No way."

"There's some people after me because they think . . . We'll it doesn't matter what they think. Point is, the good guys, they don't know where my dad is. They think he might be involved with the bad guys, and they probably wouldn't be happy that I was talking to him."

Kip narrowed his eyes. "Then why are you talking to him? That sounds dumb."

"Maybe. But I'm not so sure my dad did the things they think he did. And he lives in Pacific Palisades, so I figure he's got the dough to help me with my knee."

"Oh-kay, but what if he's the bad guy those good guys think he is?"

"That's why I need you to come with me. I figured they wouldn't do anything to you. And I also thought you could text Megan the address and tell her to send it to your dad and Mr. S if we're not back by eight."

Kip folded his arms. "Just what kind of bad guys are we talking about here?"

"I don't know. Spy stuff."

"Seriously?"

"Yes. Kip, please. I'm not making this up."

"You think your dad was a spy that went rogue, like Jason Bourne or something?"

"I don't know. Maybe." But I liked the sound of it. Maybe my dad wasn't the traitor. Maybe someone in the Mission League was.

"I still don't believe you," Kip said, "but I'll drive you down there. It's just too crazy to pass up."

And with that vote of confidence, we snuck out the back door and into Kip's Bimmer.

He backed into his neighbor's driveway, then turned out to the left. I watched over my shoulder until we passed through Pilot Point into Burbank and got on the 134 headed west. We'd done it. Kimball and Mr. Sloan weren't behind us.

If only I could be certain that was a good thing.

We made excellent time until we reached the 405. Traffic inched along that freeway no matter the time of day, but it was five o'clock, which was the middle of rush hour, so it was extra bad. By the time we reached the Getty Museum, we'd come to a complete stop. I pulled out My Precious II to find an alternative route and saw that Sue Adams had left me another message.

"That reporter woman will not give up. I don't know what she wants me to say. I'm out for the season? I'm sure Coach told her that."

"She just wants to be the one to chronicle your rise to fame and fortune," Kip said.

"Maybe she should wait until I get there." I typed in the address my dad had given me. "Take Sunset. We'll drive over the mountain."

The exit lane moved faster than the freeway and curved west onto North Church Lane. My gaze snagged on the sign pointing toward UCLA. I swear that place was haunting me. But at the next intersection, we turned west on Sunset, leaving my dream school behind us.

This section of Sunset was two lanes of traffic each way that cut through a residential neighborhood with lots of palm trees on both sides of the roads. We passed through Brentwood Village. When we rounded some of the corners, the setting sun was blinding. We eventually entered Pacific Palisades. Houses got fewer and farther between. The road got curvier, the hills steeper. Large homes rose up on cliffs to my right, down the cliff to my left. I kept looking for Evans Road, but didn't see the sign.

My phone said we'd gone too far. "We passed it."

"Where?" Kip said. "There were no roads."

He swung onto Will Rogers State Park Road and turned around. We headed back up the hill on Sunset. On a big curve, I spotted a turn lane. "There." I pointed. "Get in the turn lane."

"It doesn't look like it's going anywhere." But Kip pulled into it and flipped on his blinker. On the other side of the road, what looked like a narrow, unmarked driveway slipped into the forest. Kip caught a break in traffic and turned. The road was barely wide enough for two cars. It was smooth asphalt, no lines. At first it ran through nothing but forest, then we passed a huge gate on our left. Another hundred yards and a gate on the right. Then the road bubbled out around a mansion sitting in a curve of the road like it was on an island.

"Dang," Kip said. "And I thought my house was big."

We didn't find my dad's address until the end of the street. And it was only the beginning of a driveway with a black iron gate blocking the way. Kip turned into the drive. A call box on top of a car-window-level pole stood on the driver's side of the gate. Two miniature bottles of Evian sat on top. Kip stopped the car, rolled down his window, and pressed the button.

"Yes?" a male voice said through the speaker.

"Yeah, this is Spencer Garmond here to see his dad." Kip looked at me and shrugged. I shrugged back.

"Pull up to the front of the house," the voice said.

The gate started to roll aside. Kip grabbed the bottles of water and tossed one to me.

"Really?" I asked.

"That's what it's for. Thirsty guests." Kip accelerated through the gate and down a freshly paved drive. Bright green hedges lined each side, perfectly trimmed. The drive gave way to a round decorative concrete courtyard in front of a Spanish-style mansion. Palm trees towered above, their shadows stretched long over the concrete. This was more than just a house. This was an estate. Sprawling green lawns stretched out on either side of the place. Behind the right side of the main building, I could see a tennis court and—

"Look at the basketball court!" I said. "Sweet."

"Who *is* this guy?" Kip asked.

"Supposedly my dad." Supposedly. And maybe a bad person.

"Great, but what's he do for a living?"

Good question. "We're about to find out."

Kip stopped in front of the house and shut off the Bimmer. We both go out. The front doors, each two halves of an arch made out of glossy wood, loomed at the top of a half-dozen red clay steps. They were also smack in the middle of a fat turret, like some sort of castle. One side of the doors opened, and a man stepped out. He was dressed in a sharp black suit, and while he didn't look older than forty, he was completely bald.

"Your padre?" Kip asked.

"Don't know. Never seen him before."

"Crazy," Kip said.

I hobbled up the steps on my crutches. When I reached the top, I saw that the bald guy was wearing an earpiece.

He held out his hand, and I tucked my crutches into my armpits so I could shake.

"I'm Richard Locke," he said, "estate manager. Pleased to meet you, Mr. Garmond and . . ." He looked at Kip, eyebrows raised.

"Kip Johnson."

"Mr. Johnson, yes, of course." Locke shook Kip's hand.

"Welcome to The Sanctuary, gentlemen." He opened the front door. "Please, come inside."

Kip and I stared at each other, then grinned. The Sanctuary was the name of the castle where the Light Goddess lived in the *Jolt* movies. How cool was that?

I hop-jumped through the open doorway and felt like I'd entered a palace. The ceiling of the foyer went all the way to the roof where a massive chandelier hung. The floors were hard white and shiny, maybe made of marble. I'm not up on my interior decorating terms, but everything looked expensive.

When Kip got inside, Locke shut the door behind us. "If you'll both follow me."

He moseyed across the foyer. A fat staircase curled along the tower wall. And the floor was sprinkled with a dozen statues of half-naked people without arms. We trailed the guy past a dining room on our right that had a table with twelve chairs and drapes covering all the walls. Apparently, the room was made of windows.

"What's an estate manager?" Kip asked.

"It's a fancy way of saying butler," Locke said.

"People still have butlers?" I asked.

"Oh, yes. Many wealthy individuals understand how beneficial it is to have professional help managing their property and their lives."

Clearly my dad had the money to help me out. But would he? The man might have murdered my mother in cold blood. And here I was in his house. You'd think I'd have learned my lesson about walking into traps. I just didn't think I'd have much of a life without basketball. Maybe that was melodramatic of me, but it was how I felt. I needed to get the best surgery possible.

Kip's and my sneakers scuffed over the floor as Locke led us through an archway at the back of the foyer and down two steps into a fancy, sunken sitting room. Everything was black and white like a real-life chess game. The far wall was all windows, open to a swimming pool, and divided by a double fireplace. I could see right through the center, over the logs and out to the pool. Awesome sauce.

A half circle of white sofas faced the fireplace. There was a TV built into the wall above the hearth. Glossy black coffee tables and end tables here and there. A baby grand in the corner. A thick red and black rug over most of the white marble floor.

"Please sit and make yourselves comfortable," Locke said. "I'll let Mr. MacCormack know you're here." And the butler left.

"*MacCormack?*" Kip said to me in a low voice.

"Yeah, Ving MacCormack is what he goes by on Facebook. That's not his real name though." Just like Spencer Garmond wasn't my real name.

"Yeah, but . . ." Kip raised his eyebrows. "The Sanctuary? Pacific Palisades . . . ?"

"What?" Kip was hinting at something that, clearly, I was too dumb to grasp.

"Who directed the *Jolt* movies, Spencer? Hello?"

"Irving Ma—MacCormack." No way. "No way!"

Kip huffed, a big smile on his face. "I don't know if you're pulling my leg about that whole witness protection thing, but this place is money. Those movies are money."

So Kip and I sat there, awed over the décor and the mere idea of Kip's hunch.

"Mr. Garmond and Mr. Johnson," Locke said.

At the sound of his voice, I turned my head to where he stood at the top of the two steps to the sunken room.

"May I introduce Mr. Irving MacCormack."

Kip stood up, like he was in trouble or something. I reached for my crutches.

A soft voice said, "Please, don't get up." A man walked past Locke, down the steps, and straight towards where I was sitting. He wasn't what I was expecting. Me, six-foot-four with freckled skin and orange hair. I'd expected someone more like me or Kimball.

But this guy was shorter than Kip, maybe five ten. He looked like he'd gone to Harvard or something. Maybe it was the paisley pattern on his button-up short-sleeve shirt, the thick creases down the front of his beige slacks, the way the ceiling lights reflected off his shiny brown shoes, or the way his black hair was slicked back over his head.

He held out his hand to shake. I accepted. His handshake was firm. Hand a little sweaty, but so was mine.

He sat beside me on the sofa and pulled me into a one-armed side hug. "It's great to finally see you face-to-face, my son. To talk with you. Thank you so much for coming."

His eyes were glossy as if this was emotional for him. I felt nothing. Okay, that's not true. I felt . . . awkward. None of this seemed real. Maybe I'd wake up on the couch at Kip's house any moment and this would have been a weird dream.

MacCormack released me and motioned to the sofa beside mine. "Please sit, Mr. Johnson."

Kip sat, staring at the man, eyes wide. Locke remained standing in the archway to the room.

"Let's waste no time before discussing your needs," MacCormack said. "You reached out to me, so clearly this is important to you."

I felt like a leech, coming for money. I decided to be honest about it. "I want to play college ball, but I don't think the surgeon at St. Vincent's is the best man for the job."

"I'm sure any surgeon would do his best," MacCormack said.

"Yeah, but let's just say, I'm not convinced this guy's best is good enough." Man, that had sounded cocky. I couldn't help it, though. This was my career. My life.

"I see your point," MacCormack said. "Yours is an injury that can't be trusted to just any surgeon—at least not with your aspirations. After we hung up, I made a few calls. If you're interested, James Landry is willing to take care of you."

I glanced at Kip. "The guy who worked on Alcott Moss?" My voice did a high-pitched squeaky thing. Landry had done knee surgery on more than one of the Lakers over the past decade.

"Yes. And many other well-known athletes. His offices are here in Los Angeles. He'd like to see you this week to schedule the surgery. I hope I didn't overstep my bounds. I was anxious to see that you receive the best possible care."

Wow. "Uh, no. That's cool. But, uh, there's a bit of a problem. I already have a surgery scheduled with that guy from St. Vincent's. Also, I didn't tell Grandma about you and I—"

He lifted his hand, palm facing me. "Say no more. You're wise to keep our visit a secret for now. If you'll tell me the name of your surgeon and your appointment time, I'll have Mr. Locke take care of it."

I looked to where Locke was standing at the top of the steps and wondered if the guy was packing. "The surgeon's name is Dr. Kapitankoff," I said. "I was supposed to go in Monday the twentieth. Of February. I can write it down."

"That won't be necessary, Mr. Garmond," Locke said. "My memory is quite good. If it's all right with you, sir, I'll take care of this right away."

"Thank you, Locke," MacCormack—err, my dad—said.

So weird.

Locke walked away. To "take care of it."

"Are you Irving MacCormack the director?" Kip asked.

The man smiled, and his teeth were so white, they glowed. "What gave it away?"

"Besides that fact that you live in a mansion called The Sanctuary?" Kip said.

MacCormack chuckled, and we laughed with him. He seemed like one of those people who everyone wanted to suck up to. He laughs, we laugh. Funny or not.

"You're too shrewd for me, Mr. Johnson," he said. "Are you boys fans of the films?"

"I'm planning a Jolt Revolt." Kip gasped and floundered a bit for words. "You—d-d-do you know Brittany Holmes?"

A slow grin filled MacCormack's face, and he turned it on me. "Would you like to meet her?"

Um . . . duh. "Sure."

"Me too," Kip said. "I want to meet her too."

"You know what?" MacCormack said. "Why don't you boys come to the premiere next week?"

"The premiere of *Jolt IV*?" Now I *knew* I must be dreaming.

"I'd love for you to be my personal guests. It'll be at the Dolby Theater. Where they host the Oscars. I'll have Locke give you tickets and see that you're put on the list. You can meet

Brittany there."

"We can meet Brittany," I said to Kip, grinning.

"Is that the one in the mall?" Kip asked.

"On Hollywood and Highland, yes. It starts at six, but you should come a half hour early."

"Could we have *three* tickets?" I asked, thinking of Megan. "Kip has a girl—"

"No," Kip said.

"What? Why not?"

"Shut up," Kip whispered, then raised his voice. "So, Mr. MacCormack, how'd you get into making movies? You go to film school or something like that?"

"No. After my first wife died"—he glanced at me—"I moved out here, got hired on a film crew. I worked my way up to directing and eventually started my own studio."

First wife. "My mother?"

He put his hand on my shoulder and looked into my eyes. "That's right."

My face flushed. Would I finally get the truth? "What happened to her? They said you killed her."

MacCormack took a deep breath. "That's not how it happened, Son. I was set up."

"By who?"

He shook his head. "I never found out."

"Come on. Then what have you been doing all these years? Why aren't you trying to prove your innocence?"

"I did try. I failed. Life isn't always like the movies. Sometimes the bad guys win."

I searched his eyes, trying to figure out if he was for real. I didn't see any signs that he was lying. But he'd been trained as a field agent, so he probably knew all those tricks.

"Your mother was an amazing woman. I never could have hurt her." His eyes were glossy with tears. "I tried to find out who did it, but I hit dead end after dead end. Son, whoever did this, they covered their tracks. All the evidence implicates me. And they have enough to convince a jury."

"Excuse me, sir."

We all looked to the entrance of the room. Locke was standing at the top of the steps.

MacCormack sniffled. "Yes?"

"The matter with Mr. Garmond's surgery has been settled. Mr. Landry's office will contact Alice Garmond regarding the changed appointment."

"Excellent. Thank you, Locke."

"Of course, sir. And, when you're ready, dinner is served."

MacCormack looked back to me. "We good?"

Uh, not really. Even if I bought his story about Mom, there was still the fact that he'd ignored me all my life. But I was going to stay on his good side for now. Get me a new knee and an introduction to Brittany Holmes. Then I'd pull the abandonment card. See what he had to say. But not yet.

So I shrugged, which was enough to get him off my back but wasn't an admission of anything "good."

"Then let's have dinner." MacCormack stood and fetched my crutches. He turned back to me and held out his hand.

I grabbed hold and let him help me up. "Thanks."

I took my crutches, and we went to the dining room, the same one we'd passed on our way in. The table was now set with white dishes, crystal glasses, and three times as much silverware as a guy like me could ever learn to use. The curtains were open, and the room really was made of windows. It was darkish out.

A woman was sitting across the table and didn't get up when we arrived.

"Gentlemen, meet my wife, Diane," MacCormack said.

Second wife? I checked her out. She looked mid-forty, had chin-length blonde hair with black highlights that made it look striped, and was wearing a silky white shirt, a pair of frameless glasses, and a strand of fat pearls around her neck.

"Hey," I said.

She smiled at me. "It's lovely to meet you."

Her voice was really high, like she had mouse DNA, and I didn't like her smile. It looked fake. And her teeth were fluorescent white too, which kind of creeped me out. Wicked stepmother or just my imagination?

Locke pulled out the chair at the end of the table, and MacCormack sat down. Then Locke pulled out the chair to MacCormak's right, the seat across from Diane. "Mr. Garmond?"

"Yeah, okay." I took my crutches in both hands and propped them against the table, then sat. I couldn't bend my leg in its brace and my foot hit something under the table. Diane shifted and glared at me, so I twisted my chair so that my leg angled away from her feet.

Locke helped Kip into the seat next to mine, then picked up my crutches.

"I need those," I said.

"I'm just going to set them in the corner," Locke said. "I'll return them when you're ready to leave."

"Oh, okay. Thanks."

"Fancy table," Kip said to Locke. "Do you cook too?"

"No, sir. Mrs. Corbett is the MacCormack's chef."

"Mr. Locke derives great satisfaction from setting the

table," Diane said. "It always looks magnificent."

"I usually eat out of a microwavable plastic tray on the sofa," Kip said. "But it gives me great satisfaction too."

I snorted a laugh, but at Diane's glare, sobered quickly.

"Tonight we're having apple and bacon stuffed pork chops with parmesan roasted potatoes, and asparagus. Does that sound acceptable to you both?" Locke looked from me to Kip.

"Sounds great," I said.

"I'll have two." Kip grinned. "Kidding. One is fine."

"I see. Could I get you gentlemen something to drink? Soda, lemonade, wine, beer? We have everything."

"Do you have hot cocoa?" Kip asked.

"Certainly."

"I don't want that. I was just wondering," Kip said. "I'll have a beer."

"No, he won't," I said.

Kip raised his eyebrows at me. "I won't?"

"One beer and you're a giggling moron. And I can't drive your car with my knee."

"Fine." Kip glared at me. "I'll have a root beer."

"Make that two," I said.

"And I'll have a Utpoia," MacCorkmack said.

"Very good, sir," Locke said. "Can I get you anything else, madam?"

"Thank you, no. I'm good with my coffee." Diane slid her middle finger around the lip of her coffee cup. She had long, claw-like fingernails, like Isabel's, that were painted light pink.

Locke left us.

"I invited the boys to the premiere next week," MacCormack told Diane.

"What a marvelous idea." She seemed to already know

who we were, and if she didn't, she didn't ask. "And the after party?"

"Of course, you both must come to the after party as well," MacCormack said.

Oh, yes, I was so there. "How late will it go?"

"Who cares?" Kip said.

"Grandma won't want me out past nine on a school night," I said to him.

"I understand," MacCormack said. "If you can't stay for the party, perhaps you—"

"We're staying for the party." Kip flashed an "I will kill you" look my way. "We'll work it out."

"Ah." MacCormack glanced from me to Kip to Diane in a moment of uncomfortable silence. He cleared his throat. "My dear, Kip tells me he's hosting a Jolt Revolt."

"Wonderful!" Diane said. "The Jolt Revolt campaign is vitally important to our cause. It's the best way to reach the masses."

"What cause?" I asked.

"The Free Light Youth," she said. "We believe in young people. And the FLYs help teens everywhere find a voice in this world."

"That's the club Brittany is a part of," Kip said. "I had to join FLY to host a Jolt Revolt."

"You make it sound like we twisted your arm, Mr. Johnson," Diane said.

"Not at all," Kip said. "There's never any arm twisting when Brittany's involved."

MacCormack chuckled.

Locke wheeled in a fancy cart covered in silver domes, which I soon discovered were covering our plates of food. He set a glass of ice and an open bottle of root beer before Kip and me, then went back for our plates. Before he set mine down, he picked up my fabric napkin and draped it over my lap.

The food was *amazing*. I bounced my good knee all through dinner to keep from moaning with every bite.

"I have a friend who's an NBA scout," MacCormack said to me over dessert, which was chocolate cheesecake so rich that when I finished it, I wanted to lick my plate.

"Cool," I said. He probably knew the President.

"I realize that your accident might turn off some of the coaches that are interested in you, but I think my friend could help. He's the agent to several Heat and Lakers players."

"Wow, thanks," I said. "That's awesome, but, uh, it's against the rules for agents to talk to high school students."

"Against what rules?" Diane asked as if the mere idea of rules was ludicrous.

Rich people apparently didn't have rules.

"NCAA," I said.

"Oh, I didn't know there were rules," MacCormack said. "Well, if you'd like to go to some Lakers games, I have season tickets on the floor behind the bench."

"That would be awesome." I'd been to plenty of Lakers games with Kip and his dad, but we always sat pretty far up. Sitting on the floor behind the bench . . . Drool.

And on it went like that. I started to get the feeling that MacCormack was trying to impress me. Or buy me in some way. Or it could be he was trying to make up for lost time. I still didn't know how I felt about that. I mean, don't get me wrong, I was getting a new knee and going to the premiere of *Jolt IV*—are you kidding me?—but the other stuff . . .

I didn't know. I just didn't know.

REPORT NUMBER: 7

REPORT TITLE: I Apply Gabe's Three Rs to My Life and Come
Up Short
SUBMITTED BY: Agent-in-Training Spencer Garmond
LOCATION: Harris Hall, The Barn, Pilot Point Christian
School, Pilot Point, California, USA
DATE AND TIME: Wednesday, February 8, 5:53 a.m.

GRANDMA DROVE ME TO SCHOOL on Wednesday. Since I
got my permit, she usually let me drive when we went places.
Now that I'd hurt my leg—and even though it was my left leg
and Grandma's Lincoln was an automatic—she probably
wouldn't let me drive for a year.

Morning League went by without too much horror.
Everyone asked how I was, but other than that, no one said a
thing. I knew they all thought my basketball dreams were over.
But these people *so* didn't know me at all.

I could still do this thing.

The rest of the school wasn't so tactful. The moment I
crutched my way into the junior hallway, I was mobbed by
"concerned friends." I used quotes there because none of these
people really looked concerned for my health. The ones who

didn't really know me looked more like rubbernecks seeing an accident on the freeway. The others were hangers-on who were worried that their might-be-famous-someday athlete friend had lost his chance.

Trella the Troll gaped at my leg. "Oh my gosh! What happened?"

"No. No!" This from Desh, his bulldog-like face scrunched up more than usual. "What have you done?"

"Please say this is a joke," Mike said.

"I'll be fine," I told them.

"But he's out for the season," Kip said, appearing on my left with Megan glued to his side.

"Says who?" Desh asked.

"Says a torn ACL," Kip said.

Desh swore and kicked the bank of lockers.

"There goes the state championship." Mike looked like he was about to get sick.

I knew the feeling.

Trella was still staring at my knee. "How'd you do that, anyway?"

"I fell off a mountain."

Desh narrowed his eyes. "Why were you on a mountain?"

"How long do you have to wear a cast?" Trella asked.

"It's not a cast," I said. "It's just a brace."

"Oh, well, a brace is nothing, right?" She grinned like everything was magically okay. "That should heal in no time."

"Try a year," Kip said. "He needs surgery."

Desh swore again.

"Does it hurt?" Megan asked.

"Sometimes," I said.

"Garmond."

We all turned around. Coach Van Buren was standing outside the door to the teacher's lounge.

"Step inside?" He held the door open.

I glanced at Kip, then crutched across the hallway and into the lounge. I'd never been in there before. It was just a big classroom with round tables and chairs instead of student's desks. It also had a few soda machines and a fridge and microwave.

Coach pulled out a chair and motioned for me to sit.

I sat and tipped my crutches against the table.

He looked down on me and sighed. "You're killing me, kid. I'm glad you're okay. Alive, I mean. You know what I mean. It could be worse."

I looked at my leg brace. "Not much worse."

"Yeah." He pulled out the chair beside mine and sat. Sighed. Rubbed his hand over his face and leaned back, staring at me as if he wasn't the one who called this meeting and didn't know what to say. Then finally, "Torn ACL, huh? For certain?"

"Yeah."

"Kid . . ."

"I know."

"I'll have to tell the coaches. I mean, I won't go out of my way to tell them, but I can't keep it from them either. They'll want to know why you're not playing."

I took a deep breath. "I know."

"I want you to still come to practices. And the game tonight."

Aw, nuts. "I don't know, coach. It sucks."

"I know this is a disappointment, but your being there will help the guys."

"It's too depressing. I'm not going to let this beat me,

Coach. But this year . . . It's over for me."

"Life isn't all about you, kid. You're part of a team. And your team needs you. We still have the skill to do this thing without you on the court, but we—"

"Gee, thanks."

"Stop feeling sorry for yourself and listen to me. You're the general. They guys look to you. We can't have you on the court, but we still need you."

"Coach, you're not serious. We can't take state now." I didn't mean to sound conceited. But we'd been winning the important games by under ten points. And I averaged sixteen, not to mention my rebounds and assists. Chaz couldn't do what I could do. There was no way.

"Guess we might as well just cancel the rest of the season, I suppose, since our star is injured."

"Come on. That's not what I meant."

"Either you're part of this team or you're not." He stood up and slapped my shoulder twice. "So I'll see you at practice."

• • •

Tonight's game was at Bell-Jeff, so I didn't have to do much thinking about it. When the team got on the bus that would take them to the game, I got in Grandma's car that would take me home.

"You sure you don't want to go to the game?" Grandma asked me. "I could drive you there."

"I'm sure." If Coach hassled me, I'd tell him Mario wanted me to elevate and ice my knee tonight to keep the swelling down or something. I just couldn't deal with this right now.

She put the car in drive and steered the Lincoln out of the

parking lot. "I got a phone call today."

Congratulations? I glared out the window at some middle schoolers playing ball on the court behind the school.

"I don't want you to worry, but they changed the date of your surgery and assigned a new doctor."

I perked up. "Who is *they*?"

"The insurance, I suppose. The man on the phone gave me the new doctor's name and the time of the appointment."

"When is it?"

"The twenty-second. That's a Wednesday. It's not going to be at St. Vincent Medical Center anymore either. It's now at the UCLA Orthopaedic Surgery Clinic. And your doctor is going to be Dr. Lundry or Laundry."

"Landry." No way. This was really going to happen.

"You're heard of him?"

"Yeah. He's good. He's real good." And so was my dad. Maybe everything was going to be okay. In time.

Grandma sighed and smiled. "Well, that's an answer to prayer, isn't it?"

Answer to prayer . . . answer to lies and manipulation . . . Such a fine line for me these days.

"Hey, Grandma?" While I was lying, I might as well keep going. "Kip . . . He got these tickets to a movie premier. It's a pretty big deal. I was wondering if I could go?"

"What movie and when?"

"It's next Tuesday night. For *Jolt IV*."

She groaned. "You know how I feel about those movies."

"Yeah, but, Grandma. We're supposed to get to meet the actors. It would be so amazing."

"His father is taking him, I assume?"

"I don't know. I think so."

"Well, as long as there's an adult with you at all times, and you come home right after, I guess it will be okay this once."

"Thank you, thank you, thank you," I said, a little shocked that she'd said yes.

"I still don't like those movies." She turned into our driveway and shut off the car. "But I think you've had enough disappointments for a while."

"Thanks." I felt like mud for lying to her, but it was Brittany. I mean, come on. I could *not* let Kip go without me.

After dinner, Kip texted me to let me know they beat Bell-Jeff 70-63. It should have been by a lot more. I didn't think I could watch my team lose everything we'd worked so hard for because of me. I don't know why Coach even wanted me there.

I went into my room and turned on my MacBook. Once I was online, I Googled Irving MacCormack. He was all over the place, of course. I found several pictures of him with Brittany Holmes.

I wanted a picture with Brittany Holmes.

I got distracted for a half hour clicking on pictures of Brittany, dreaming of what I'd say when I met her. My Facebook bleeped. I clicked over and saw a message from my dad.

Surgery should be all set. See you soon.
Dad

I clicked around his Facebook page for a bit, but he didn't have any activity. Not even a profile picture. I clicked back to my Google search, admired the last picture I'd found of Brittany, then did a new search for Irving MacCormack.

This time I avoided pics of Brittany or anything having to

do with Light Goddess movies and just focused on Ving. I don't know . . . My dad was supposedly a wanted man. As famous as Irving MacCormack was, you'd think someone would have recognized him by now. Unless he'd changed his appearance drastically.

Last year, I'd found some pictures of my mom in Grandma's bedroom. I had her pale skin and nose. She'd been blonde. Maybe my red hair had come from my grandpa or something. Kimball had it.

I looked like Kimball.

I looked nothing like MacCormak.

And MacCormack looked nothing like Kimball.

It suddenly struck me as ludicrous that Irving MacCormack could be my dad—could be Kimball's brother. Even if he had dyed his hair and got contact lenses.

I read MacCormack's bio on Wikipedia. No trouble with the law listed. And he gave loads of money to charity, but that was probably to help himself on his taxes. There was no mention of me, but it did say, "He was married briefly out of college."

I didn't know what to think. I mean, what kind of guy who claims to love his kid abandons him to save his own hide?

What would Gabe say to that, now that he was a card carrying M.A.N?

The question made me grin. WWGS? Maybe thinking about what Gabe would say or do was a good tactic to keep myself out of trouble. Gabe would not have climbed down that cliff face to hide. He also wouldn't have lied to his grandma in order to meet a famous actress. And he wouldn't have ditched his team like I had.

All I could remember from Gabe's man party was that a

man should be respectful, responsible, and righteous. Thinking about those things made me realize something.

I *had* abandoned my team. I didn't mind being the guy who fell off a cliff because he wasn't thinking or the guy who lied to meet a famous actress. But my team . . . my sport . . . it meant everything to me. And I'd just left them like none of it ever mattered. That had been selfish. And totally irresponsible.

Tomorrow I'd start going to practices again. Because that's what players did. Besides, my team needed their general.

● ● ●

I had my consult with Doc Landry the next morning—he said to call him that. Before he could accept me for surgery a week from next Wednesday, I needed to gain full movement in my knee. That meant attending physical therapy every day so I'd be ready. When I mentioned that I knew a freelance physical therapist—Mario from C Camp—Doc Landry said I could work with him.

See? Everything was going to be okay.

In the car, on the way back to Pilot Point, I called Mario. Since there was no way I could get down the steps in Harris Hall, I wasn't going to be attending morning Mission League for a while. Instead, I'd meet Mario at C Camp for my physical therapy.

Grandma dropped me off at school. It was lunchtime, so I hobbled into the cafeteria on my crutches and joined the guys at our usual table.

"Hey! How'd it go?" Kip asked, bumping Megan down the bench to make room for me on the end.

"Good." I lowered myself onto the seat, then twisted my

legs under the table, leaving my left one straight. "You know my surgeon worked on Kobe?"

"That's amazing. Coach say anything about the colleges? Arizona still in?"

I sighed. "He hasn't heard anything. But I'm coming to practice tonight."

"That's cool," Kip said.

"Baby, I'm going to get some Jell-O," Megan said. "You want some?"

"Nah."

Megan left the table, and Kip leaned close. "Dude, I need you to tell Megan I've got to help with your physical therapy tomorrow night. It's Valentine's Day, and she wants me to take her out."

Valentine's Day? I hadn't realized. "Why don't you want Megan to come with us?" It was the premiere of a famous movie. I'd think it would have earned Kip some serious brownie points on Valentine's Day.

"I'm not bringing my high school girlfriend to meet a hot actresses. I want Brittany to think I'm available."

"Puh-lease. Like she'd give you the time of day."

"We'll see," Kip said. "You just wait. I'm better at this than you think."

I didn't doubt Kip had a gift for picking up girls. What I doubted was his gift for picking up *famous* women. "Why don't you break up with Megan if you don't like her?"

"I want to keep my options open, okay?"

WWGS? I asked myself. The thought made me chuckle.

"What?" Kip asked.

"Nothing." But I couldn't help but notice that Kip had none of Gabe's three Rs going for him. He'd always been a dog where girls were concerned. I used to think it was funny. Now I wasn't sure. Megan didn't deserve being treated like this.

But that was really none of my business. I was going to practice tonight to try and undo *my* mistakes.

Kip was going to have to take care of himself.

• • •

I crutched my way into the gym after school. Some of the guys were shooting around, but not everyone had arrived yet. Coach saw me and jogged over.

"Garmond! How are you?"

"Good. I met my doctor today. James Landry." I kept a straight face and watched him for a reaction.

He met my gaze. "Sure you did."

"I'm not kidding. I've got to do physical therapy every morning until next Wednesday to get my knee ready. Then I go down to UCLA at eight a.m. for the surgery."

"How did you get Landry? Seriously."

I shrugged. "The office called Grandma." Not a lie, but it wouldn't hold up against the three Rs.

"Look, I'm just going to come out and say it," Coach said. "ASU pulled their offer. They're still interested, but they want to wait and see how your fall looks. See if you've healed. The fact that Landry is doing your surgery should help keep that conversation going."

I took a deep breath. "And the other schools?"

"Not a word. We're just going to have to wait and see."

Great. But dwelling on it wouldn't change it, so I might as well stay on task. Tomorrow night we had our last game of the season, then next week was the Southern Section playoffs.

"Anything I can help with today, Coach?"

"Yeah. Would you mind working with Chaz? He doesn't rebound as well as I'd like."

And so I spent half the practice giving Chaz tips on how to improve his rebounding. And I think he was doing a little better by the end of practice. Then they started scrimmaging, so I spent some time working with Jonathan, a freshman swing player who had a nice outside shot. With a little more practice, he'd be a great three-point shooter.

Friday night Coach had me dress and keep my warm-ups on for the last season game against Heritage. That way he could have me on the roster.

"Won't that just mess up my season stats?"

"Your stats are toast now anyway. But if any college coaches are paying attention, your being here shows that you care about the team, not just yourself."

"I *do* care about the team."

"I know. You wouldn't be here if you didn't."

We won the game 96-39. It was weird watching the game from the bench, knowing I wasn't going in. But I wouldn't have played much in a game like this, anyway, since Coach liked to let the second string and JV swing players get some game time. Next we needed to focus on the Southern Section playoffs.

The weekend flew by. Kip was with Megan, so I stayed home. I texted Grace to see if she was ever coming back. I kind of wished I could get that pathetic text back the second I sent it, but oh well. No answer yet.

And then it was Monday night and I couldn't sleep because tomorrow was Tuesday, Valentine's Day, the day I would meet Brittany Holmes.

I hoped.

REPORT NUMBER: 8

REPORT TITLE: I Walk the Red Carpet and Meet a Famous
Actress
SUBMITTED BY: Agent-in-Training Spencer Garmond
LOCATION: Kip Johnson's House at 733 Elm Street, Pilot
Point, California, USA
DATE AND TIME: Tuesday, February 14, 4:38 p.m.

AFTER PRACTICE, KIP DROVE US TO his place to get ready for the premiere. While he was in the shower, I sat on the edge of his bed and pulled out my grandpa's old retro suit. I'd rolled it up and stuffed it in my backpack that morning and now it looked pretty wrinkled.

"You're wearing *that*?" Kip said, walking in the doorway wearing a towel. "Your homecoming suit?"

"It's all I've got. Premieres are supposed to be formal."

"Yeah . . ." He eyed the wrinkled fabric, then shrugged. "You might get away with it, actually. Those Hollywood types love the word *vintage*."

"I thought it was retro," I said. "What's the difference?"

"Is there one?"

I shrugged. "I don't know. What if some reporter asks me,

and I say the wrong thing?"

"No reporters are going to talk to us, man. Look, you're going to have to iron that thing, or wear something of mine."

"I can't wear your clothes." I was too tall. And too buff.

"The iron's in the laundry room."

I pushed to standing and grabbed my crutches. "Can you help set it up? Please?"

So Kip led me to the laundry room, put down the ironing board, and plugged in the iron. "Do you even know how to use an iron?"

Oh yes. One of Grandma's favorite punishments was to make me iron quilt squares. "I think I can manage."

Thirty minutes later we were in Kip's Bimmer, heading into Hollywood. The traffic was bad, but thankfully we didn't need to get on the freeway. And we had plenty of time.

We parked in the garage under the mall on Hollywood and Highland and came up the escalators. But the way to the theater was blocked off with huge fake walls. A security guard told us we had to go out front and enter on the red carpet.

Sweet.

A ten-foot wall, plastered with the *Daystorm* movie poster, had been erected along the north side of Hollywood Boulevard. When I saw the actual red carpet, I about died. It covered the two north-bound lanes of the street, probably about eighteen feet wide. A metal barricade separated the south lanes, which were lined with bleachers and packed with fans. Hundreds of people were standing against the barricades too, five or six deep, waving posters and DVDs and headshots of Brittany, Valeria, and Dennis.

Kip and I made our way to the entrance of the red carpet, and I almost got taken out by a black Audi convertible that drove right up on the carpet. The fans screamed—not in terror. They were excited. Sure enough, Dennis Wylde got out, held his hands above his head, and waved. He jogged around his car and opened the door for his date—some chick I'd never seen before, who was wearing a slinky black dress. She got out. Dennis grabbed her, dipped her over backwards, and kissed her.

The fans went nuts.

Dennis escorted his lady down the carpet and waved at fans, stopping every five yards to pose for photographers. No autographs from the guy Brittany was likely going to kill in the movie.

The guys always died in these *Jolt* flicks.

Some dude in a black suit jumped in Dennis's Audi and drove it off the red carpet. Kip and I inched up to the entrance.

Another black-suit guy flew up in our faces. "This street is closed to pedestrians."

"Do we look like pedestrians to you, fool?" Kip said. "Spencer, give me the tickets."

I dug them out of my pocket. Kip grabbed them and waved them in the guy's face.

I really hoped we didn't get arrested before I got to meet Brittany Holmes.

The black suit glared at Kip and snatched the tickets out of his hand. His expression instantly softened. "Hey, Brooks!" He waved a bald guy over and gave him our tickets. "Take these two to check in."

Brooks grinned at us. "Right this way, gentlemen." He motioned for us to follow him.

And that was how we entered the red carpet walk. Kip waved at the crowd, which made them scream. I hobbled along beside him on my crutches. The reporters seemed to know we were nobodies and ignored us.

I needed me some bling crutches, that's what.

"How long you been doing this?" Kip asked our guide.

"A few years."

"You ever wave at the crowd?"

Brooks chuckled. "Um, no. Paychecks are nice."

"But you don't care if I wave?" Kip asked.

"Not at all."

So Kip waved again. But that was his last chance. We came to a gold and velvet rope barrier that stretched along the ten-foot high wall, creating two paths: a fifteen foot one for the stars and a three-foot one for people who no one cared about.

That was us.

I was thankful that Sue Adams from the *Pilot Point Bulletin* didn't cover the Hollywood scene. She was still trying to get me to talk to her about my injury.

But I didn't want to think about that right now.

I pulled out My Precious II and snapped a picture of Dennis and his girl, who were posing for the paparazzi. Wish I would have thought to get a picture of him and his car.

We soon left Dennis in the dust. When we neared the entrance, I could see the El Capitan Theater above the bleachers across the street. The crowd was screaming for someone else. Brittany, I hoped.

I scanned the red carpet and marked Valeria Silver, one of the co-stars of the franchise, surrounded by three guys dressed in black. Valeria played Brittany's BFF and demon hunter wing-woman. She was cute where Brittany was gorgeous. Tinker Bell compared to Wendy. Valeria was wearing a short, strapless white dress that was covered in hairs. Or feathers. I wasn't close enough to tell the difference.

Valeria strutted down the carpet five yards at a time, stopping to pose for pictures and wave. The men in black, ear pieces in place, moved with her. Must be bodyguards.

Our guide turned off the red carpet, through a break in the fake walls, and into the actual mall. Everything was shut down here as well.

"Where are we going?" I asked.

"To the check-in tables. Hopefully whoever gave you these tickets will have put your name on the list."

"Tickets aren't good enough?" I asked.

"Not for a *Jolt* movie. Where'd you get them?"

"Ving MacCormack," I said, trying to sound like he and I were BFFs.

"Ah, then your name is likely on the list. Mr. MacCormack's staff is very thorough."

Brooks led us to the table where a handful of twenty-somethings, dressed like he was, were looking bored.

"Jessica, hello," Brooks said, handing our tickets to a pretty girl with a ponytail and a black suit jacket and skirt. "I have brought two ticket-holders that need to be checked in."

Kip winked at Jessica. "Kip Johnson."

Why was he talking? "It will be under Spencer Garmond," I said.

Kip glared at me until Jessica said, "Ah, Spencer Garmond, here you are. Personal guest of Irving MacCormack. Lucky you." She smirked at Kip. "And you must be Mr. Garmond's plus one."

I laughed out loud at that one.

"Gentlemen, enjoy the film," Brooks said.

Jessica gave us lanyards with a metal tag on the bottom. It

had a picture of Brittany from the movie trailer with the words *"Jolt IV: Daystorm"* on the top and "VIP ACCESS" on the bottom.

I took a picture, then hung it around my neck with so much reverence, I may as well have just won me an Olympic Gold Medal for basketball.

Jessica pointed us to the theater's entrance, which was only about ten yards from the table. Halfway there the wall ended and the red carpet came into view again. Dennis and his girl were still out there, posing for tomorrow's Yahoo! Entertainment News headlines.

Outside the doors to the theater, a crowd of people were mingling. Guys and girls in back with little white aprons were walking around with trays of hors d'œuvres and something bubbly in stemmed glasses.

Kip snagged a glass as a waiter passed by and sipped it. A slow grin crossed his face. "Champagne."

"Really?" I looked for another waiter. I wanted one.

"Spencer!" MacCormack appeared at my side, with his wife Diane just behind him, and squeezed my shoulder. "So glad you could make it. And your friend. We'll sit together inside, of course."

I nodded, grinned at Diane, who was giving me her usual glare, then caught sight of Valeria Silver's white dress just over Diane's shoulder. Valeria and I . . . we made eye contact. I'll never forget that moment. Meeting the sultry gaze of a famous actress, then watching as she smiled and walked toward me.

Me.

She was two steps away when MacCormack pushed past and embraced her. Gave her the Hollywood kiss-kiss on each cheek.

Should have known she hadn't been looking at me.

But then . . . "This is my son, Spencer," MacCormack said. "Spencer, meet Valeria Silver."

Now I *know* she was looking at me. "Hey," I said.

"My, you're tall!" She elbowed MacCormack. "Might want to take a paternity test on this one, Ving."

Ouch.

Ving just laughed. "His mother was a supermodel," he said. "And he's going to play NBA."

I got to say, I liked his introductions.

"Ooh, I love basketball," Valeria said.

"I'm Kip." He stepped between us, grabbed Valeria's hand, and kissed it. His impersonation of Dennis Wilde, perhaps? "Do you believe in love at first sight, Valeria Silver, or shall I walk by again?"

Here we go.

Valeria barked a deep laugh, then looked Kip up and down. "Walk by all you want, honey. I don't mind the view."

I'm sorry, what? Would no one *ever* slap him?

Kip moved closer to her. "So when are you going to get your own movie, girl? Because you shine."

"Oh, Ving. I like this one," Valeria said. "Can I keep him?"

But Ving and Diane had walked away. With them moving on and Kip flirting with Valeria, I felt a little lost.

And then I saw her. Brittany Holmes, Light Goddess, strutting this way, parting the crowd like she was dressed in fire. She was wearing a flimsy orangish red dress that draped over her body like a bed sheet.

Yeah, I know. Mind out of the gutter. Three Rs and all that. I shook my head a bit to clear it. Brittany stopped to kiss-kiss MacCormack, then Diane. She laughed at something MacCormack said. She was wearing lipstick the same color as her dress, and her hair was down and curly and wild and—

They turned my way. They were stepping toward me. I suddenly couldn't remember who I was or why I was here. The sound around me dipped. My head got dizzy.

"—my son, Spencer."

"Nice to meet you, Spencer." Her face was looking up into mine. Wild black hair. Red lips. Gleaming teeth.

What was it with rich people and glowing teeth?

"What's with the crutches?" Brittany asked me.

I just stared, trying to think of something clever to say.

"Torn ACL," I heard Kip answer.

She tilted her head to the side, making her curls swing in one big clump. "What's that?"

"It's a ligament in your knee," Kip said. "Spencer has a ton of offers to play college ball. And he's going pro after that, Lakers, hopefully. But first he's got to get back in shape."

"He looks like he's in fine shape." And I swear she checked me out.

"Oh, sure. Spencer can bench his own body weight. But he's got to work his knee. It's tough physical therapy. But Kobe came back, and so did Rondo. So I have no doubt we'll be watching Spencer on TV someday."

Mental note to thank Kip for making me look cool despite my crutches and sudden case of muteness. I just about worked up the courage to say something, but then Brittany looked at me, raised one sculpted eyebrow, and pursed her lips like she might blow me a kiss.

"So tell me, Spencer. Does a torn knee ligament injure your tongue?"

"Ah . . . no."

She tipped back her head and laughed.

"I think he's just trying to find the words to propose," Kip said. "It's challenging to get that just right."

She swung her hair Kip's way. "He's a fan, then? Is that it?"

"We're both your biggest fans ever. In fact, I'm hosting a Jolt Revolt party in a few weeks in Pilot Point."

"Oh, excellent, Kip!" Brittany Holmes reached out and grabbed Kip's arm. Touched him—that punk. "That's so good for the film and the FLYs."

"Sure. Hey, you know what would make my Jolt Revolt the best? If you and Valeria dropped by."

Did Kip just invite Brittany Holmes to his lame high school party?

But she clicked open her little purse, which looked like a mini black football, and pulled out a cell phone. She handed it to Kip. "I won't promise anything, but put in your number and maybe I'll call you."

"Me too," I said, suddenly able to speak. I pulled out *My Precious II* and held it out to her.

She smirked at me. "Oh, no, Mr. NBA. You give *me* your number. I don't give mine to anyone. Nice suit, by the way. Who made that?"

"It was my grandpa's." What? No! What was the matter with me?

She tipped back her head and laughed again. I loved when she did that. I'm an idiot, but at least I'd made her laugh twice.

MacCormack leaned into our little circle. "It's time to go in."

Kip handed Brittany her cell.

I reached out to take it first, but she slipped it back into her football purse before I could get my hands on it.

I whimpered.

"No worries," Kip whispered to me. "I put your number in."

"My new one?"

"1575, yes."

"Thank you." And then it hit me, the past two minutes of my life. I took a deep breath. "Dude."

"*I know*," Kip said. "You're welcome. And guess what? Valeria gave me her number."

I pushed a crutch at him. "Shut up."

"Ooh, hold up, there." Kip put his empty champagne glass on a waiter's tray, grabbed two full ones, and handed one to me. "Now you see why I didn't bring Megan?" He took a long drink.

"I guess." Megan still wouldn't be very happy if she found out. "Hey, no more of that. I can't drive your car."

"The movie is two hours long. Then there's a party. I'll be fine. Drink yours. You need to loosen up. What if Brittany talks to you again?"

Point taken. So I downed the champagne and gasped at the way the little bubbles tingled in my ears. Nice.

I handed Kip the glass and crutched my way into the dark theater. Nothing fancy about this place on the inside. The theater was open for regular movies all week. Kip and I had seen *Star Trek: Into Darkness* in here.

I sat on MacCormak's left, Kip sat on my left, then some random guys filled out the row. Brittany and Valeria were a few rows behind us. Dennis was sitting in the row ahead.

On the bright side, with Brittany back there, I'd be able to watch the movie instead of staring at her all night.

Though I might do that anyway.

The lights went down and everyone applauded and cheered.

Roll film.

REPORT NUMBER: 9

REPORT TITLE: I Insult Brittany Holmes: Light Goddess
SUBMITTED BY: Agent-in-Training Spencer Garmond
LOCATION: Dolby Theater, Hollywood and Highland Center,
Hollywood, California, USA
DATE AND TIME: Tuesday, February 14, 6:07 p.m.

THE MOVIE OPENED WITH A GUY, maybe fourteen, wearing Civil War era knickers and a poufy white shirt and vest. He was walking through a field of waist-high grass. He lifted a wooden mask to his face and tied it in place, stumbling a bit as he did.

Numbers flashed at the bottom of the screen: 1843.

It was twilight, and in the distance, an old, southern mansion sat on a hill. The lights were on, making all the windows bright orange.

Suddenly the boy was knocking on the door. It opened, revealing a man in a fancy old suit, who was wearing a sculpted tin mask that covered his eyes and cheeks but left his nose and mouth bare.

"Yes?" the man said.

"She walks in beauty, like the night," the boy said.

The door opened wider, and the boy stepped inside. The man shut the door and walked deeper into the house.

The boy followed.

They entered a rectangular room, no windows, no furniture. There were hundreds of candles on wall sconces, pillars, the floor itself. Ten men in two rows were sitting cross-legged on the wooden floor, facing each other and creating an aisle from the door to the other end of the room where two pillars and an altar stood.

The man who answered the door walked between the sitting men and, when he reached the altar, turned. "Kneel."

The boy knelt.

"Do you declare upon your honor, before these witnesses and me, your Grand Master, that you freely offer yourself as a candidate for the mysteries of the Daysman?"

"I do, sir."

"Have you chosen a name?"

"Degory Freeman."

"Behold our sanctuary, young Master Freeman. It is good and pleasant for brethren to dwell together in unity, is it not?"

"Yes, sir," the boy said.

"It is freedom," the other men chanted.

"Freedom, yes." The Grand Master went to the altar, picked up a pipe, and lit it. He took a long puff and held it in for a moment as he walked forward and handed the pipe to the nearest man on his right. Then he exhaled a plume of smoke. The one now holding the pipe took a drag and passed it down the line.

"In the beginning God created the heavens and earth," the Grand Master said. "Darkness was upon the face of the deep. But God said let there be light. And there was light."

"Light is freedom," the men chanted.

The Grand Master walked back to the altar and picked up a thin white candle. He carried it to the boy and held it above his head. "My brother, I present to you this candle as an emblem of but one source of light, a representation of all you have within you, and a distinguished badge of a Daysman. Guard it well."

"It is the light," the men chanted.

The Grand Master handed the candle to the boy.

"The Daysman have four levels of consciousness. The first is called Sleep. One sleeps in a bed, vulnerable, innocent. One might dream. And the Daysman has been known to visit the Sleeper there. Some dreams are forgotten, but some are remembered. Watch for the Daysman in your dreams."

"Sleep is the light," the men said.

"The second level of consciousness is called Sleepwalking. One appears to be awake, walks around, goes to school or work, does chores, sings, entertains. Yet one is merely in a walking sleep, ignorant of the spirit world around him. The Daysman can visit the Sleepwalker, as can a follower, for this is how Sleepwalkers become enlightened."

"Sleepwalking is the light," the men said.

"The third state of consciousness is called Seeing. One partakes of connection and is granted sight."

I perked up at the word "connection."

On screen, the man was still talking. "He sees himself as he truly is: a prisoner in a mortal shell. The experience of Seeing often gives one the opportunity to see and speak with Osbert Leofdaeg, the first Daysman. Only a Seer can pass on to the fourth, and highest, level of consciousness."

"Seeing is the light," the men said.

"The fourth level of consciousness is Understanding. When one asks the Daysman to unleash the power within, one is set free from his mortal shell. One sees all creatures as they truly are, some free, some still trapped in their mortal shells. Thanks be to Osbert Leofdaeg, the first Daysman, who will give to any who ask, the power within, the power to be free, to be an Understander."

"Understanding is the light," the men said.

The phrase "power within" made me shiver. What was it with these movies and the Bratva stuff in Moscow, anyway? Creepy.

The last of the seated men puffed on the pipe and returned it to the Grand Master who handed it to the boy. "Will you partake of connection?"

Now see? See? That sounded just like Bratva. I still hadn't heard back anything on the reports I'd written last summer about the Light Goddess movies and their similarities to the Bratva cult. Maybe I'd just have to investigate this myself.

The boy took the pipe. "I will." He put it in his mouth and sucked in a long breath. He coughed and hacked. Hands shaking, he handed the pipe back to the Grand Master.

"This is the Dawning of a new day. From this day forward, you will know a freedom unlike any other."

"Freedom is light," the men chanted.

"O Daysman, master of the light," the Grand Master said, "we present to you a new follower. Come into this Sleeper's life and unleash for him that which he seeks: the power within!"

"The power is light!" the men yelled.

"Repeat after me. 'Sleeper of Light, I pledge my service to you.'"

The boy repeated the line.

"To the Daysman!" the men shouted.

"'Light, stream to my mind,'" the Grand Master said.

The boy repeated the line, and this time the men joined in.

"'Descend down to earth, give power to my heart, and give my life worth.'"

The boy repeated the line along with the men. His vision was starting to blur.

I wondered what was in that pipe.

"'Light, guide my will. Daysman, show the way, to harness power and live the Daysman way.'"

Light flashed near the ceiling of the room. Wind blew, whipping the men's clothing back. A man appeared, standing between the Grand Master and the kneeling boy. The man wore scarlet and gold robes, like some Roman Emperor. He was white, with short, curly white hair and a beard.

The boy cowered at the man's feet, eyes wild through the holes in his mask.

Then the apparition spoke. "Welcome, Degory Freeman. You are the creator of your life. You are the father of your destiny. You have unleashed the Light. All power comes from within you."

"The power is in you!" the men yelled over the crackling of the wind.

The boy screamed. Then light shot out from the boy's mouth, eyes, fingers, toes, and formed the title credits on the screen: *Jolt IV: Daystorm.*

The audience cheered, which made me jump. I'd been so into the scene I'd forgotten I was at the premiere.

The screen went black. The words "Present Day" flashed in white text.

The camera settled on a close up of Brittany Holmes's

face. The audience cheered and whooped. This time, I did too.

"Let's go!" Brittany said. She looked over her shoulder. Valeria sprinted toward her, some ugly thugs on her heels.

"Faster!" Brittany yelled.

Valeria pulled a grenade from her utility belt and threw it behind her. It exploded in a shock of orange flame and black smoke. Thugs' bodies went flying.

The audience cheered again.

The Light Goddess rolled her eyes. "That works too."

The girls had just defeated a powerful demon and stolen his talisman, which held great dark power. Brittany needed to dispose of it fast.

They made it back to The Sanctuary, where Brittany got an email from her European counterpart, Véronique, who said a storm was coming, hence the movie's title: *Daystorm*.

And so Brittany and company had to jet off to France to join forces with Véronique's squad and take on a storm of evil.

Pretty wild stuff. And the best movie yet.

When the credits started to roll, we all went upstairs to the after party. The room was about half the size of a gymnasium and shrouded in pale pink light. Low, square benches made of fuchsia leather and as big as full-size mattresses were scattered around the room. People could sit on all four sides. Even lower white square tables sat around them, covered in candles and trays of munchies. And every so often there was a fat recliner-like throne make of red fur.

Happy Valentine's Day.

Windows covered the far wall, and I could see the round Capital Records building in the distance.

Kip and I stayed with MacCormack, who introduced us to all the stars—so cool. And everyone was super nice to us, probably because we were with the director and they were sucking up to the boss, but whatever.

Eventually MacCormack and Diane wandered off to talk to someone else. Kip grabbed another glass of champagne. I wanted to punch him, but Valeria was standing two feet away.

"How many is that?" I asked and Valeria looked at me, then Kip.

"I'm not drunk, Spencer, though I might be intoxicated by Valeria's beauty." He said this loud enough for her to hear.

She stepped toward us. "Kip, someone as charming as you must have a girlfriend."

"Naw, but I do know a girl who'd be mad at me for saying that."

She chuckled. "Oh, you are a handful, aren't you?" She propped her hand on one hip and slouched, striking an alluring pose.

"Careful, precious," Kip said, "so many curves and me with no brakes."

I rolled my eyes and hobbled over to a red fur throne chair that was within reach of a tray of goodies. Looked like some kind of toast with soft cheese and tomatoes, but I was starving, so I ate two at once and fell into the chair, which was tall enough to lean my head against the back. I sat there by myself for way too long, trying not to glare at Kip and Valeria. I didn't see Brittany.

Would things be different if I wasn't hurt? Probably not. I couldn't do what Kip did. Words got stuck in my throat whenever girls were around. It took me a while to work up to saying anything worthwhile.

I heard my name from somewhere behind my chair and strained to listen.

"The basketball kid?" Brittany's voice. No way!

"That's right." MacCormack answered. He was talking to Brittany about me!

"And what's my goal?" Brittany asked.

"Make him fall in love with you."

Wait, *what*?

She chuckled. "I've already accomplished that much. He couldn't even speak to me. Tongue-tied in my presence."

Yeah, but I hadn't been prepared.

"You know what I mean, Brit. I need you to own this kid. Do whatever it takes to make it happen. To make him happy."

"Not a problem. Where is he?"

Holy figs!

"I don't see him," MacCormack said. "That's his friend there with Valeria. He's probably in the bathroom."

"Then I'll wander that way and see if I can bump into my new boy toy."

"Thank you, my dear."

"Anything for you, Ving."

I sat there in shock, replaying what I'd heard. Brittany drifted past my throne, and I watched her walk toward the far wall.

Boy toy?

I felt betrayed. And I didn't exactly know why. Was this another way MacCormack was sucking up to me? From his tone, I didn't think so. He had ordered her to own me. Own me. What was *that*?

I fumbled for my crutches and stood. I didn't want to be sitting there when she came back.

I hobbled toward Kip and Valeria. Across the room, Brittany disappeared into a hallway that must lead to the bathrooms.

"Kip." I swallowed and raised my voice. "Kip, can I talk to you a second?"

He looked at me—glared was more like it. "Dude, there's nothing you could possibly offer me that's half as attractive as what I'm already looking at."

Valeria giggled and swatted his arm.

"Now. Please?"

"Can't it wait?"

"Twenty seconds."

Valeria leaned close to Kip. "I've got to talk to Dan, anyway. Come find me later."

"I'll miss you."

She chuckled and walked away, Kip's eyes following her as she went.

I held my crutch under my arm and punched his shoulder. "I just overheard MacCormack tell Brittany Holmes to do what it takes to make me happy."

That got his attention. "Shut up."

"Dude, I am *so* not lying. MacCormack thought I was in the bathroom and sent her over there to find me." Just then Brittany stepped back into the party. Her head turned slowly as she panned the room. Her eyes locked onto mine, and she walked toward me. "Oh, man. Here she comes. What do I do?" I hobbled to the nearest mattress bench and sat down.

Kip sat beside me, but his eyes were on Brittany. He looked back to me, brow furrowed. "Whatever she wants, fool. Why are you even asking?"

"But I don't understand. Why would he do that? And why would she?"

"Who cares? Spencer, if you screw this up, I'll hate you

forever."

"Oh, real helpful."

Brittany sidled up then. "Hey, boys." She beamed like she was in a lipstick commercial. "Mind if I join you?"

I stared at her so hard my eyes started to water. Ten minutes ago I would have done anything for this woman. I would have eaten cockroaches and walked through fire, been buried alive and dog paddled through a pool of maggots.

But now?

She may as well have been one of Anya's minions.

Which meant my dad was a bad guy.

Duh?

I slipped my fingers under my necktie and felt through my shirt. The tender wound on my chest that was still healing.

The mark of my faith?

"We were hoping you would," Kip said, patting the seat beside him.

I couldn't remember what she'd even asked. But Brittany sat next to me, so close that her right arm went around my back and her side pressed up against my arm. She smelled like fire and flowers all at once. And the neckline of her dress was gaping so much that I could see, well, lots.

"Life is so unfair," Kip mumbled.

Tell me about it.

"You want to get out of here, Spencer?" Brittany asked.

My gaze lifted to her eyes then fell down to those red lips. If I leaned toward her, would she kiss me? Right here? Because MacCormack had told her to make me happy?

"MacCormack tell you to say that?" I asked.

Her eyes widened, then she grinned and bumped her shoulder against mine. "Okay, how did you know that?"

"Spencer's psychic," Kip said.

"Oh yeah?" Brittany reached across her lap with her other hand and set it on my thigh. "What am I thinking right now?"

I fought back a whimper. "That you have to do whatever it takes to make me love you." Figs and jam. Why had I said that? I sounded like a pompous jerk.

This time she frowned. "You heard us talking."

"Do you always do whatever he tells you?"

"Spencer, *shut up*," Kip whispered.

Brittany sighed, like she was *so* bored, then looked up at me, blinked her über thick lashes a couple times. "He's my boss."

"Yeah, but what you described is more like a pimp." Oh no. Had I *really* just said that? Really?

She clicked her tongue and stood. The air conditioning chilled my leg where she'd been touching me. She spun around and glared down. Her silky orange skirt fluttered around my knees. "I make people happy, *little boy*. You don't want to be happy, fine."

Oh no. Brittany Holmes was mad at me. What had I done?

Kip stood up. "I want to be happy."

But she walked away. *Stormed* was more like it, her shoes clack, clack, clacking over the hard floor.

Kip swore. "I can't believe you."

I grabbed my crutches and stood up. "Let's get out of here."

"Um, no way, José," Kip said. "I am not leaving until this party is over."

I sucked in a short breath. "Then I'll take a cab."

Kip and I stared at each other, long and hard. He broke eye contact first. "Have a nice ride." And then he walked away too.

So I headed for the exit. What else was I supposed to do? I'd ruined everything with my big mouth.

This was why it was better not to speak.

On my way out of the party room, my left crutch got stuck in the glass door. I was fighting with it when Brittany Holmes came and rescued me.

"Look, Spencer. Sorry I lost my temper. How about I text you sometime and maybe we can go for coffee. Does that sound okay?"

She was babying me. I'd basically called her a hooker and she was offering to get together. What kind of power did MacCormack have over this girl?

But I nodded. I mean, I was *so* thankful that she'd thrown me a second bone. I hated that I'd insulted her. I wanted to beat myself up. Why couldn't I be like Kip? What was the matter with me, anyway?

"Okay, give me a hug." She slid her arm around my waist and bobbed up on her tiptoes and kissed my cheek. It was like pressing up against fire that couldn't burn. She fell back to her heels and grinned up at me. "Goodnight, Spencer. Until next time."

"G'dnut," I croaked, then cleared my throat and tried again. "Goodnight." I stood there for a good ten seconds before I remembered that I was the one leaving. Right.

I turned on my crutches and vaulted myself toward the elevator, two yards at a time.

I'd just made it inside when Kip ran up and stopped the doors from closing. "Dude, you're really going to turn her down?"

"Yeah," I said, acting like I rejected hot movie stars every day.

"You're an idiot."

He was right. I felt stupid and small and passed over, though I'd been the one doing the insulting. "So *you* say."

"Well, if you don't want her, you don't care if I go for her, do you?"

Really? "You have a girlfriend."

"So? Stop bringing it up. She's not your sister."

"It's wrong."

"It's none of your business."

"You should respect her, that's all."

"Respect her? What does that even mean?"

For Kip? I had no idea. For me? I guess I was just starting to figure it out. "Just . . . break up with Megan if you want to go after Brittany or Valeria or whoever."

"Like I'd take advice from a guy whose longest relationship lasted six days."

"Whatever," I said. "You staying?"

"Yeah. You leaving?"

"Yeah."

And Kip let the elevator doors close. It took me a while to find my way outside. It was dark and all the red carpet stuff had been taken down. I crossed the street and sat on a bench outside the El Capitan. I pulled out *My Precious II* and called Gabe. Kimball was likely somewhere nearby since Kip and I hadn't bothered trying to ditch him tonight, but I didn't want to answer his twenty questions.

"Hey, what's up?" Gabe said.

"I need a ride. I'm sitting outside the El Capitan."

"What are you doing down there?"

"Does it matter?"

"Maybe."

"Gabe, come on. It's your fault I'm here. An actress wanted to take me out, but all I could think was your flipping three Rs. So get down here and tow my crippled butt home where I can cry in privacy."

"I'm on my way."

So I sat there, watching an Asian Captain Jack Sparrow, a female Michael Jackson, and a creepy-looking Mickey Mouse try and get tourists to pay to pose for pictures.

Then it hit me. Holy figs! What did I just do? If I went back right now, maybe Brittany would still take me out. I could tell her I was embarrassed or something. Intimidated. Yeah, that should work. A girl like her probably liked having guys groveling at her feet.

Girl like her.

God, why do you torture me? I mean, really.

Really.

REPORT NUMBER: 10

REPORT TITLE: My Best Friend Steals My Dream Girl and
Gets Dumped
SUBMITTED BY: Agent-in-Training Spencer Garmond
LOCATION: C Camp, 95 Juniper Avenue, Pilot Point,
California, USA
DATE AND TIME: Wednesday, February 15, 6:07 a.m.

"THESE ARE REAL SIMPLE RANGE OF motion exercises that you need to do before and after surgery," Mario said.

It was just after six Wednesday morning, and Mario and I were the only two people in the C Camp building.

Mario was a muscular guy with dark hair and skin and a wide smile. He reminded me of Mark Sanchez.

"We need to get that knee bending again, but we also want to get the swelling down and get the cord muscles working."

So Mario taught me a bunch of exercises: ankle flex, bridging, glute sets, hamstring curls, heel raises, heel slides, quad sets, standing shallow knee bends, and two types of leg raises. I was supposed to do a minimum of three reps of ten, three times a day. But Mario said the more I did, the better.

Then he got me on a stationary bike, but when I tried to

pedal the thing, I couldn't.

"That's okay," Mario said. "Just rock it back and forth, back and forth. Every day you'll get a little farther, okay?"

"Yeah." So depressing though.

"Hey, it can be discouraging, I know. Try and stay positive. You know what might be fun?"

"Fun? I have no idea."

"You have that YouTube channel going for your basketball, yeah?"

"Yeah."

"Why not post videos about this? Show yourself working hard, your physical therapy and everything. Could be those college coaches won't care. Could be they might, though. And could be you help someone else who's dealing with this, you know, so they know they're not alone."

Mario was a little too peppy sometimes, but the idea had merit. I mean, it couldn't hurt. At least I'd be posting something on that page. "I'll think about it."

● ● ●

Kimball gave me a ride to school in the sedan with him and Mr. Sloan. They didn't seem wise to my time with MacCormack. And I hadn't told anyone about the convenient location of the stitches on my chest, either. I probably should, but I just wanted to wait until my knee surgery was over.

By the time I hobbled my way to my locker, Kip was already there, waiting for me. Without Megan.

"You still ticked at me?" I asked.

"Nooo." Kip grinned, fought it back, pursed his lips until he had a straight face. "I think I love you, actually."

Uh oh. He had big news. "Why the change of heart?"

"Because you left Brittany all alone and rejected and someone had to comfort her."

No. "Shut up."

He shrugged. "If you don't want to know what happened, I'm sure Desh and Chaz would love to hear it." He turned like he was going to walk away, but looked over his shoulder, eyebrows cocked, waiting for me to stop him.

A knot grew in my chest, right behind my heart. I didn't want to know. I didn't. "Spill it. Now."

"Because I'm so afraid of a guy on crutches."

"*Kip.*"

"I went home with her. To her massive mansion house in Beverly Hills. And we smoked some pot and made out. I would have stayed the night, but my dad texted and said he was putting out an APB on me if I wasn't home in a half hour. But we're going out again on Friday after the game."

The pressure in my chest had grown. The knot was now a dull ache. "Sure you are." He was lying, right? Right?

"I'm not lying. And I have the pictures to prove it." Then Kip pulled out his phone and blessed me with pictures of him, Brittany, or part of both their faces, sitting on the floor in front of a couch, smoking a rolled up joint, laughing.

"She's, like, thirty," I said, because I didn't know what else to say. I seriously wanted to hit something. Maybe Kip.

"Twenty-two. Looked her up on IMDB this morning." Kip squinted at me. "You're mad. You said I could."

"I'm not your mother." I slammed my locker, settled my backpack over one shoulder, and tucked my crutches under my arms. Then I hop-stepped it toward our homeroom class.

Kip walked alongside me. "You said you didn't care."

"What happened with Valeria? I thought you liked her?"

"Are you kidding? I'm in love with both of them. But Valeria started hanging with some guy who looked like a boxer. So I found Brittany and . . . You know me."

Yeah. I did. "Does Megan know?"

"No. But she's mad I didn't text her back all night."

What if Kip and Brittany started dating? What if I started seeing pictures of them on the covers of magazines?

Please no.

That could have been me.

Stop. Don't be dumb. Say something normal. "Uh . . . Think I can come to your house tomorrow after practice? I wanted to do a *Jolt*-a-thon. Watch the first three movies." I needed to take notes on all that connection stuff so I could write up another report.

"Why not tonight?" Kip asked.

"Uh, practice? Quarter-finals? Mission Prep? Hello?"

"Right," Kip said, looking at his phone again.

"Dude. You need to pay attention. The team needs you."

He pocketed his cell and scowled. "Don't start with me."

"We lost the Rock Academy tournament last year because you just had to go off with the cheerleaders. And then you guys attacked Grace."

"That was Desh. Not me. Stop freaking out." Kip slowed outside the door to homeroom. "Wait. Is that why you rejected Brittany? Grace?"

"No. I just wanted to know why MacCormack told her to do that. And why she would. Did she say anything to you?"

He grinned wide. "She said lots of things. But we weren't talking about you."

I wanted to destroy him. "Shut up."

Kip cackled and strode into the class. I wished I could go home and weep, but that, sadly, wasn't an option.

• • •

We won the Southern Section quarter-final game against Bell-Jeff that Friday night, 70-63. Sue Adams from the *Pilot Point Bulletin* cornered me and finally got the answers she'd been so desperate for. Yes, I was disappointed that the schools had pulled their offers. No, I wasn't giving up. Yes, it was true that Dr. Landry was doing my surgery. Yes, I'd be playing this fall. No, I didn't know if the schools would still be interested. Yes, I hoped they would.

The following Tuesday, we had the semi-final game against Buckley. That was a tough game, but the guys worked hard, and we managed to win, 55-52.

Then came Wednesday, February 22, the day of my surgery. My "dad" had Facebooked me a few times since the premiere last week, but I hadn't answered. And I almost confessed the whole mess to Grandma on the drive to UCLA Orthopaedic Surgery Clinic. I mean, if MacCormack was somehow involved in a cult like Bratva, maybe he worked for Anya. And if he worked for Anya, I'd be an idiot to go under the knife of a surgeon Anya had connections with.

But Doc Landry's reputation spoke for itself. He wasn't a quack. He'd worked on so many famous athletes, I was sure he wouldn't risk his reputation botching surgeries for cult leaders.

That didn't keep the doubts out of my head that morning, though.

By the time I was sitting in the pre-surgery bed, my heart was pounding, my palms were sweaty, and my stomach hurt.

Of the three types of surgeries available for a torn ACL, I'd chosen the hamstring surgery. It should give me the best change at a full recovery and had the lowest percentage of re-tearing. A nurse came in and hooked me up to an IV. Grandma and I stared at each other awkwardly for about an hour until the anesthesiologist showed up and gave me a shot in the back, which numbed me from the waist down. So weird. I kept trying to move my legs, but it was like they weren't even there.

Then Doc Landry came in. "How are you feeling, Spencer?"

"Just want to get it over with so I can get back on the court."

"Then let's do this."

They wheeled me to another room—one Grandma wasn't allowed in. And the next thing I knew, it was over. I think I fell asleep. Who knows what they put in that IV drip bag. I woke up in a recovery room. My leg was all wrapped up in gauze and Ace bandages and a fat brace. Grandma showed up to check on me a half hour before Doc Landry did.

He said everything went smoothly, and if I was patient and kept up with the physical therapy, there was no reason that I couldn't be back on the court in nine to twelve months.

I needed nine. Eight, really.

That night Grandma took care of me. She brought me meds and fresh ice on a regular basis. But I was pretty much a groggy mess. Sleep was the only thing I wanted then.

Not even a date with Brittany.

• • •

The Southern Section Final game was Friday, February 24 at

Mater Dei High School in Santa Ana, which was about an hour south of Pilot Point. Ours wasn't the only game that day. The section finals for Division 4A and Division 6 schools, both boys and girls, were being played there too. Our game was at 3:30 that afternoon. We'd be playing Mission Prep.

When the guys were warming up, I took a seat on the end of the bench and put my crutches on the floor under the chairs. We'd beat Mission Prep twice in season games—by at least ten points both times. But I'd been playing then. Tonight would be harder. But this was a team we could beat. I knew it.

We got off to a great start. Chaz got some passes to Desh, who was bigger than all their forwards. We led 21-11 at the end of the first quarter. Then Kip got into something with their guard. I hadn't seen what started it, but they were throwing elbows and hips and looked seconds away from throwing fists. Kip got his third foul and coach took him out.

By halftime we were only ahead by six. Coach and the guys took off for the locker room, but I wasn't fast enough to keep up. By the time I got there, Coach's voice had lowered to a grating lecture, but I could tell by the look on everyone's faces that I'd missed a major tongue-lashing.

The guys headed back out to warm up. All but Kip and Coach, who were talking.

"He needs to be put in his place," Kip said.

"Maybe," Coach said, "but so do you."

And when the third quarter started, Kip was sitting beside me on the bench. Strangely, I would have thought that benching Kip was a sure way to lose the game. But Alex went in and, in less than twelve seconds, sank a three pointer.

"Great," Kip grumbled. "Now he'll never put me back in."

"I'm sorry, is your being in the game more important than

that three points?" I asked.

Kip didn't reply. It was interesting, watching the game from my perspective, knowing I couldn't play. For the last few weeks, I watched my teammates for their own personal strengths, not for how I could use their positions to make things happen on the court. And Chaz really was a good ball handler. He couldn't rebound, and he didn't make steals, but no one could steal from him. And he had a great left-handed drive. I'd never noticed that before. Next practice I'd see if I could help him learn to keep his eye on the ball on defense.

Mission Prep fought hard but never got closer than six points. We won the game, 60-54. Things got a little crazy then with everyone jumping in a mob out on the court. I tried to get out my crutches so I could join them, but there were too many people, streaming off the bleachers. So I just sat on my chair and cheered and tried to keep my leg out of people's way.

Sue Adams found me there and asked me a bunch of questions. I tried to get her to go talk to Chaz or Desh, but I guess she was just enamored by my awesomeness.

Winning the section finals was a pretty big deal. Tonight's win qualified us for the state tournament and earned us the first seed for the Southern Division. That would give us a bye for the first game in the state championship bracket, which was nice. But we still had another four games to win before that trophy would be ours.

When I got home that night, I did my physical therapy exercises, then looked up pics of Brittany online and felt sorry for myself because she hadn't texted me yet.

Neither had Grace.

The following Monday after practice I went home with Kip to watch the *Jolt* movies. We chatted like normal, but everything was *not* normal between us. It was like we'd both caught Awkward Disease or something.

To make matters worse, twenty minutes into *Jolt I*, Megan showed up.

"Hey, baby." Kip tried to kiss her, but she pushed him away.

"Don't you 'Hey, baby' me. Explain this?" She held up her cell phone.

I paused the movie.

"Hey, check that out!" Kip said. "Me and Brittany Holmes. Nice."

"*Nice?* That's what you have to say?"

"What? You think that's real? Spencer made that. In Photoshop. Right, man?" He turned to me, giving me a look.

Megan gave me a look too, hands on her hips, eyes on fire.

I raised my hands in the air. "I'm staying out of this."

Kip shrugged. "Well, it was one of the guys. Maybe Mike. Or Desh. It must have been Desh."

Desh, who didn't even know how to save a document? Yeah, must have been him.

The door opened then, and Kip's dad came in, wearing his police uniform. "Hey, guys. How was school?"

"Your son is a pig," Megan said.

Mr. Johnson straightened. "Really?"

"Yes, really. He cheated on me." Megan shoved Kip.

"Whoa, now. Just hold on a minute." Mr. Johnson pulled her back, then turned his "license and registration" gaze on Kip. "That a fact, son?"

"So what if it is?" Kip yelled. "Only an idiot would reject a famous actress." He glanced at me.

I smirked back and muttered, "Jerk."

Megan growled a scream. "I'm out of here. Don't call me, Kip."

"I *won't*."

She stomped out the door and slammed it behind her.

The three of us stared at the door, silent. Kip's dad was the first to speak.

"What famous actress?"

A lazy smile crossed Kip's face. "Brittany Holmes."

"Son, if you want to break up with a girl, just do it. There's no reason to make up a lie like that. It's . . . hack."

"It's *not* a lie." And he got out his cell and started showing his dad the pictures.

Unbelievable.

"Where did you meet her?" Mr. Johnson asked.

"At a party," Kip said, as if Brittany made a habit of frequenting high school parties in Pilot Point.

Mr. Johnson took Kip's phone and squinted at it. "Is that what I think it is?"

"It was just one joint, Dad. And we shared it."

Mr. Johnson took a deep breath. "Some people lace their pot with meth or crack. You could end up in a hospital. Be careful."

Be careful? Are you kidding me? That was all the man had to say? A cop? If that had been me in those pictures, my grandma would have me in rehab. And when I got out, she'd send me to that military school she'd picked out a few years back.

Must be nice to have such a laid back dad.

Mr. Johnson and MacCormak would probably get along great.

• • •

My birthday flashed by that week. I did not have a M.A.N.
party. Since my birthday was February 29, leap year, the
school did not list it in the announcements, as they did with
everyone else's birthdays. But Grandma made me a cake that
night and gave me a bunch of clothes that Kimball likely
bought. I was seventeen now. So yeah.

With the drama with Megan, I didn't get all my movies
watched and had to go back to Kip's on Saturday morning. I
asked Kimball to drive me. When I got there, Kip's dad opened
the door in his boxers.

"Spencer, hey. What's up?"

"Just coming over to watch some movies."

"I thought Kip was at your place."

"Oh. Sorry." I adjusted the brim of my Lakers' cap, feeling
stupid for not knowing where Kip was.

Mr. Johnson smirked. "Would have been nice if he'd told
you that you were his alibi, huh?"

I laughed awkwardly. "Yeah, I guess." Kip had better not
have been with Brittany, though I suddenly remembered that
he'd said he was going out with her on Friday night.

I hated myself. That could have been me.

"Well, you want to come in and wait?" Mr. Johnson said.
"Or I could have him call you when he gets back. He'd got to
set up for his party tonight."

The Jolt Revolt. "Can I come in? I really need to watch
these movies. It's for an assignment, but, you know, we don't
have a DVD player." Grandma Alice and her technophobia
anyway.

"Sure." He pulled the door wide for me.

"Thanks, Mr. Johnson." I vaulted myself inside.

"It's Doug, Spencer. Doug. Plus, I've got a guest over and don't want to hear you call me Mr. anything."

Guest? Awkward.

"In fact, could you watch those in Kip's room? Make yourself scarce?"

"Uh . . . I guess I—"

"Doug!" a woman called from deep in the house. "Are you coming back to bed?"

I blinked at Kip's dad. He waggled his eyebrows.

And I realized then that Kip was just like his dad. Mr. Johnson always had a date with some new woman. Why should Kip be any different?

"You know what? Just have Kip call me." I pinched my crutches with my pits and fumbled for the doorknob, wanting to get far, far away.

Mr. Johnson opened it for me and held the door as I exited. "I'll have him call you."

"Thanks."

I would have had Kimball drive me to Gabe's, but Gabe didn't have a TV in his room, and I didn't think Mr. S would allow *Jolt* movies in his living room. So I went to Lukas's place.

"Oh, I love me some Brittany Holmes," Lukas said. "*Ella es hermosisima.*" He popped in the first DVD. "Hey, I heard someone say that Kip is dating her. You hear that?"

"Kip makes things up sometimes." And sometimes not.

"Yeah, because that's crazy, man."

"Yeah." Crazy.

So Lukas and I had a *Jolt*-a-thon, and since he was in the Mission League, I told him that I'd heard some of these phrases on one of our summer trips, though I wasn't allowed to talk specifically about the Moscow mission.

"So connection means drugs?" Lukas asked.

"Yeah, and in the movies, they take the drugs before they call out to the Light Goddess."

"Or the Daysman," Lukas said.

"Right. The fourth movie said the first Daysman was Bert something. I can't remember."

"You saw the fourth one already? How?"

"Early screening in Hollywood. Won some tickets. So"—I took a quick breath—"there was also mention of 'power inside.' Like, releasing it or connecting to it."

"And that's what Brittany's peeps do in the movies. It's what brings the lightning down every time."

"There's definitely a connection," I said. "No pun intended."

"I think so, too," Lukas said. "You should show Mr. S."

"Come on. How am I going to get Mr. S to watch these movies?"

"Yeah, that's no good." Lukas snapped his fingers. "What if you bought the scripts? Then you could photocopy the pages and give those to Mr. S."

"Yeah, I could do that." The only question was, did I beg Grandma to help me buy the scripts online, or should I ask MacCormack for them? I wasn't sure I was ready to visit The Sanctuary again, knowing my dad was trying to get his she-minion to "own" me. "Think you could order them online if I gave you the cash?" I asked Lukas.

"Yeah, no problem."

"Thanks." At least now I had a plan.

REPORT NUMBER: 11

REPORT TITLE: I Get Kisses, a Mickey, and a Night in Jail
SUBMITTED BY: Agent-in-Training Spencer Garmond
LOCATION: Grandma Alice's House, Pilot Point, California
DATE AND TIME: Saturday, March 3, 3:47 p.m.

I WOULD HAVE SKIPPED KIP'S jolt revolt party, but he started texting me that afternoon, freaked out that no one would show. Since I'd signed up two months ago, I said I'd go. Though I don't know what I was thinking. Looking back, it must have been the painkillers that made me say yes. I should have stayed with Lukas.

A party meant a lie. I called Grandma and told her I was spending the night at Kip's and promised to be careful with my knee. Kimball gave me a ride from Lukas's house to Kip's. I felt a little weird having my former SRO drive me to a party, knowing there'd be alcohol there. But what Kimbal didn't know . . .

Plus Kip's parties never got out of hand, probably because everyone knew his dad was a cop. His dad wouldn't be there, of course. He never was. I think they worked out a deal. Whenever Kip had parties, his dad worked late. And Kip was careful to keep things quiet.

Like I said, must be nice . . .

This time, Kip tried to make the party special by playing *Jolt* soundtracks and passing out plastic Lone Ranger masks, but it was just a regular party. Brittany didn't show. And I didn't ask. He did have more than fifty people there throughout the night, so I guessed he'd earned his prize pack. I hoped he'd loan me his DVD screening copy of *Jolt IV* so I could verify some things in my report.

The moment I arrived I grabbed a spot on the couch by the wall where no one would trip over my sore leg. I did my best to keep a video game controller in my hand all night. I really didn't want to be there. I was still mad at Kip. And I could tell he was mad at me.

Jasmine showed up and instantly attached herself to my side. I guess she liked me. But whenever I looked at her, all I could think about was Grace, though they looked nothing alike.

What was wrong with me? Why couldn't I just hook up with any girl who crossed my path, like Kip or Mr. Johnson? I blamed Gabe and his three Rs.

Last night, I'd dreamed about Grace. It was the dream where I found her hurt in her bedroom. It was the kind of dream that would turn into something I'd experience in real life someday. I wondered how far out in the future it was. I'd been having the dream since Okinawa, but that didn't mean anything. I'd been having the wolf one for years. But Grace still hadn't told me when she was coming back.

When Jasmine went to fetch me more pizza, I sent Grace a text: *You okay? I had another dream about you. Please text back.*

Today was the first day since the surgery that I was

actually hungry, so I let Jasmine spoil me. She brought me food and sodas and changed the ice pack on my knee. I had my foot up on the coffee table. It wasn't a bad arrangement.

Without Megan present—or Brittany—it only took a few beers before Kip started making out with Trella the Troll. Then they went in the kitchen and started baking. They looked so happy, it almost made me want a beer.

Almost.

I couldn't play ball anyway. What was the point of toeing the line?

Truth was, I was still on the team, in Coach's eyes. And I'd made a point of being there for the guys. I was going to stick this thing out until the end.

So I sent Jasmine to get me another root beer. The girl was saving my life tonight with the way she was at my side, playing maid. If she hadn't been there, I would have caved already.

About the time Jasmine started giving me a backrub, My Precious II bleeped. A text. Grace?

Nope. It was from Mary Stopplecamp. *Where r u? Just had a nightmare that u got in trouble @ a party.*

A chill ran over me. I knew better than to shrug off a dream of Mary's. She was gifted in prophecy the same way I was. It was 1:34 in the morning. I looked around. There were only a dozen people still here. But Kimball and Mr. Sloan would still be out front. I just needed to get my crutches and they could take me home.

"Hey, Jasmine?" I turned to look up at her. "Can you get me my crutches? I'm ready to head home."

"Already? But I thought you were staying the night?"

"I was, but I'm not feeling so good. It's probably the

meds."

She stuck out her bottom lip but walked toward the front closet where Kip had stashed my crutches.

Good. It was time to get out of here.

I turned my attention back to the TV and watched Chaz attack a herd of zombies. He died almost instantly, though, and it was my turn again.

Trella passed out the brownies she and Kip had made. Brought me a five-inch square, which turned out to be two that were stuck together.

"Thanks," I said taking the gooey warmth in my hand.

"Get him, Spencer!" Chaz yelled. "Stop eating brownies and shoot them!"

I shoved the whole thing in my mouth with one hand as I tried to kill two ugly zombies that were standing in the exit of the bus station.

"Behind you, stupid!"

"Thut up!" I told Chaz, trying to chew and laugh at the same time and not choke.

Two turns later, Jasmine fell onto the couch beside me. "Open up," she said, bringing a brownie to my lips.

Keeping my eyes on the game, I bit into it, but I got overwhelmed by a herd of zombies that had been hiding in a dumpster.

I dropped the controller in my lap and let Jasmine feed me the rest of her brownie. "Wait. Where are my crutches, girl?"

"Sorry! I got distracted by dessert."

"Well, can you *please* get them for me?" I needed to hit the road.

Instead she rose up on her knees and kissed me.

Oh.

Oh wow.

I tried to come up for air a few times. "Jasmine . . . hey . . . come on . . . Jasmine . . . I really need . . . I need to go."

She wasn't hearing me.

I guess I just have that kind of effect on girls.

But Mary's warning was fresh in my mind, so I finally had to push her away. "Jasmine, I need to—"

She ran her fingers through my hair over my left ear. "If you don't feel good come lay down in the guest room."

Uh . . . "Jasmine . . ."

"Spencer, are you playing or not, man?" Chaz asked.

"Yeah." So I picked up my controller and killed some more zombies. And I was *really* careful not to die for a *really* long time.

But I was starting to feel weird. A little dizzy. Kind of high. But I hadn't drunk anything, and I didn't see anyone smoking.

The brownies.

Figs.

I ran my guy into a cave where I wouldn't get killed, then glanced at Jasmine. "Did Kip and Trella put something in the brownies?"

"Spencer, stop hiding," Chaz said. "That's cheating."

I waited for her to answer. She only smiled a little. "They said it was a surprise."

I swore for real this time. "Get me my crutches. Now."

Her eyes went wide, but she scrambled off the couch and ran toward the door.

"Desh." I tossed him my remote. "I'm taking off."

"Finally. I've been waiting to play all night."

"You played first," I told him.

"Yeah, but my turn was, like, three minutes."

"You're so full of it." I glanced toward the door and saw Jasmine talking to Kip and Trella. "Jasmine, come *on!*" I should have never let her take my crutches. I thought of getting up and hopping to the door. I thought of texting Kimball to come in and carry me out.

Instead I watched zombies eat Desh's brains. He really sucked at this game.

Chaz was up next, and by the time the zombies killed him, one walked out of the TV screen.

"What the . . .? Look at that zombie!" I said to Desh, who was taking his turn. "Did you see that?"

But the zombie was gone.

So was Desh's turn. Chaz was battling the evil zombies now.

I needed a bath. I lowered my leg from the coffee table and scooted to the edge of the couch. "Let's go to the Jacuzzi."

"Good idea!" Why was Jasmine screaming? And when had she come back? She jumped up and ran away. Maybe from the zombie.

I spotted another brownie on the coffee table and reached for it, but it was only my cell phone.

"I can't feel my arm." I turned to Jasmine, but she'd turned into a pillow. "Can you feel my arm, pillow lady?" I chuckled.

"Desh, it's your turn," Chaz said. He was wearing purple.

"You're a purple people eater," I said, laughing. "And you only have one eye."

"How many brownies did you eat, man?"

"A million." That was funny and I laughed long and hard. I should call someone and tell them how many brownies I'd eaten. "Let's call Brittany Holmes. Kip has her number."

"Kip's a liar," Chaz said, staring at the TV.

Flowers sat beside me and I leaned close to smell them. "Kip said the Jacuzzi is broken," Flowers said.

"You smell pretty."

The flowers giggled. "You think I'm pretty?"

"Dude! Something was in those brownies," Desh said. "Did you eat some? Chaz, did you? I feel weird."

"I'm not a moron," Chaz said.

"I ate a million," I said.

"Spencer, tell me I'm pretty again."

"I thought your name was Flowers."

"Guys! We need to try something," Kip said. "Come over here and sit in a circle on the floor."

"Who's making that sound?" I asked. There was a sound, like a groaning. Maybe from under the couch.

"Don't you like me?" Flowers kissed my cheek.

"I like Grace. And Brittany. But Kip stole Brittany from me, and now I have nobody. Kip steals all the girls."

"Shut up, Spencer, and get over here."

"*I* don't want Kip," Flowers said, and then she kissed me. But someone was still making noise. And I could feel the purple people eater watching us. I broke away. "Don't stare!" I told the purple people eater.

"You're wasted."

"Jasmine, Spencer, get over here!"

So I stood up, then collapsed. "Ow!" My knee hurt.

Flowers leaned over me, her hair ticked my face. "You forgot your crutches, silly."

Somehow Flowers and the purple people eater got me into the circle. The walls were spinning around us.

"It's a merry go round!" I said. "Spin it faster!"

"Guys, shut up. I need you to repeat after me, okay? Say, 'Light, stream into my mind.' "

"Kip, you're a freak," the purple people eater said.

"Spencer, look," Flowers said. "It's like we're in a car. You're driving, and I'm in the passenger's seat."

I pretended to start the engine, then grabbed the steering wheel and pressed in the clutch, which hurt my knee.

"Spencer, come on, man, say it."

"It." I cracked up and fell back on the floor, laughing.

"No, you moron. Say, 'Light, stream into my mind.' "

Flowers fell down beside me. Her lips found mine. She tasted like brownies.

"Jasmine, you're not helping. Aw, forget them. The rest of you guys, say, 'Descend down to earth, give power to my heart, and give my life —' "

The doorbell rang.

"Don't open it!"

"Why'd you open it?"

"Go, go!"

The floor shook.

Doors slammed.

"You guys, let's go!"

"Jasmine, hurry!"

"Spencer, come on!"

I pushed Flowers off me. "They're playing hide and seek."

"Spencer, you moron!" someone yelled, his voice distant.

Flowers screamed and sat up. I stared at the ceiling. It was covered in whipped cream. I reached for it.

"What's going on here, boys?" a man said. "That you behind the couch, Chaz?"

The purple people eater swore and tried to jump over the

couch. He fell. Glass shattered. The room stopped spinning long enough for me to see myself sitting on the floor, alone, staring at a pair of beetles.

"Those are huge!" I said.

The beetles moved toward me. "Spencer Garmond, right?"

I looked up to see a man's blurred face. "Do you hear that?" I asked him. "Someone is moaning. I think there's a body in the couch. You might want to — Hey! Did you know your feet are beetles?"

"You been smoking pot, Spencer?"

"Pot? Flower pot. Flowers gave me the, uh, the . . . brrroowwnniieeeesssssssss."

"Spencer, *shut up*!" the couch said.

"Stop moaning!" I told the couch. "That's *so* loud!"

"Pot brownies?" the beetles asked me.

"Troll brownies," I said. "Ooh, we should watch *The Hobbit* right now."

"Why don't you get up and come with me," the beetles said.

"Because my knee hurts. If I cut off my leg and got one of those artificial limbs like that South African sprinter, think I could play in the championship?" I asked the beetles.

"You're not playing anything for a long while, champ."

Well, that wasn't very optimistic. "I wish I was a snake, then I wouldn't need legs."

"Then how would you dribble?"

"Oh yeah." Those were some smart beetles.

● ● ●

I spent a night in the Drunk Tank at the Pilot Point Police

Station. It wasn't until the middle of the next day that I started to come down from the high, but they wouldn't release me to Grandma until I was sober enough to answer their questions. There was no blanket on the scratchy mattress in the cell. I was freezing and my knee was cramped.

Finally some officer took me to a room for questioning. Officer Barrios came in with Grandma. They were chatting like old friends. Officer Barrios was the new SRO at Pilot Point. A few years back he'd taken over for Kimball, who now followed me 24-7.

"C-Can I have a blanket?" I asked through a shiver.

Officer Barrios nodded to the officer who'd brought me in, and the guy slipped out of the room, hopefully to bring me a blanket.

Barrios asked me all kinds of questions. Who was at the party? What were we doing? Who supplied the alcohol? Who brought the drugs? Who's idea was it to put the drugs in the brownies?

The other cop brought me a blanket, and I pulled it around my shoulders. "Thanks." I told Officer Barrios that Kip and Trella had made the brownies. "I don't know where they got the pot."

"It wasn't just pot. It was a mix of marijuana and iVitrax."

I sobered up instantly. "*What?*"

"So Kip and Trella both made the brownies?" Barrios asked.

"Yeah. But I didn't know they'd put anything in them. I swear. I didn't even want to be there. I was trying to leave, but Jasmine wouldn't bring me my crutches."

"Why were you trying to leave?"

"Because Mary . . ." I glanced at Grandma. "I need to talk

to Kimball."

"Just answer the question," Grandma said. "Officer Kimball said he'd talk with you later."

Great.

"So why were you trying to leave, Spencer? You knew about the drugs?"

"No." I took a deep breath. "Because Mary texted me that she had a dream that I got arrested for being at a party."

"Mary who?"

"Mary Stopplecamp."

"One of Pat's girls? Isn't she a little young for you?"

I sighed. "We're just friends."

"And she had a dream about you?"

"Yeah."

"And that made you want to leave?"

"Yeah. Mary's dreams . . ." I swallowed. "They usually come true."

"I see. Whose idea was it to conduct a séance?"

"I don't know. What is that?"

"Calling on dead spirits," Officer Barrios said.

What? "I don't remember that."

Barrios consulted his papers. "Um . . . Does connecting to a source of light sound familiar?"

My stomach turned. "Wait. Tell me *exactly* what that's about. Where did you hear that phrase?"

Barrios leaned back in his chair and chuckled. "I'm asking the questions here, pal."

"No, please. That's . . . uh . . . It's from a movie I saw. The *Jolt* movie. *Jolt IV*. They said that in the movie."

"I knew I shouldn't have let you seen that film," Grandma said.

"No, you don't understand, Grandma. Something is bad about that movie. And it might involve the Russian mob."

"Okay, I think we're done here," Barrios said. "Seems he's still higher than I thought."

"I'm not high. I need to talk to Kimball. Or Mr. S."

"I'll be in touch if I have any more questions," Barrios said.

"Thank you, officer." Grandma stood and grabbed her purse.

"But I need to talk to them. Please. It's important."

"You'll see Mr. S soon enough," Grandma said. "I don't need to wait for the judge to tell me to put you in counseling."

What? "Grandma, come on, I don't need counseling."

But I knew there was no convincing the woman.

I was taken back to my cell for a few hours until my detention hearing, in which the public defender entered a plea denying the charges against me. My pre-trial hearing was scheduled for March 12, and I was released into Grandma Alice's custody.

I couldn't go to school. Mr. McKaffey had called Grandma while I was in jail. I was suspended for ten days. And there'd be a hearing as to whether or not they'd let me come back or expel me. I couldn't even go to the state playoff games.

And then there was that article in the *Pilot Point Bulletin* by my BFF Sue Adams, which was totally unfair. I was the only one named. Singled out. Just because I was trying to play D-I basketball. Just because she was obsessed with chronicling my every move.

I really hated that woman right now.

THE BULLETIN • SUNDAY, FE

Top basketball recruit arrested in Pilot Point

Pilot Point--A high school basketball player who's regarded as one of the Southland's top recruits has been arrested in his hometown of Pilot Point on charges of possession. Six other Pilot Point teens were also arrested.

Pilot Point PD says 17-year-old Spencer Garmond was arrested Saturday. He faces one misdemeanor charge: under the influence of a controlled substance. He has a hearing set for Mar. 12.

The 6-foot-4 point guard from Pilot Point Christian School was a rising junior with offers from Arizona State and Gonzaga when he tore his ACL in a hiking accident. He recently underwent surgery at the UCLA Orthopaedic Surgery Clinic, though it's unclear at this time if he will make a full recovery.

Arizona State and Gonzaga had no comment.

Grandma took *My Precious II* and my MacBook, so it wasn't until church on Sunday the following week that I found out what had happened to everyone else. Gabe and Isabel were onstage warming up with the worship band, but Lukas and Arianna filled me in.

"They arrested Trella and Jasmine and five of you basketball players," Arianna said. "You, Kip, Mike, Alex, Chaz. All deservedly humbled."

I ignored her snark. "What about Desh?"

"He got away," Lukas said. "Ran for it."

"Desh outran a cop?"

"That's what Jonathan was saying," Lukas said.

Who knew Desh could move that fast? Wish I'd have been coherent enough to witness it.

"Kip didn't get suspended, though," Lukas said.

"What?" How could that be?

"He'd better get suspended, or I'll file a protest with the school board," Arianna said.

"He's denying the drugs were his," Lukas said. "And he hadn't taken any."

Unbelievable. "Are you kidding me? He put them in the brownies!"

"It's his word against Trella's," Lukas said. "Kip said Trella must have snuck them in as a joke. And Trella said Kip wanted to reenact a scene from *Jolt IV*."

"It *was* a Jolt Revolt party, after all," I mumbled. "I can't believe he'd let Trella take the blame."

"Well, the police are having a hard time deciding who gets the possession charge because neither of them ate any brownies," Arianna said. "More of you corroborated the reenactment of the horror film scene, which blamed Kip, but

Trella has gotten in trouble for cooking pot brownies before."

"She has?"

"Yeah, and there's one more thing. Something I heard my dad say they found on Kip's cell phone."

"Pictures of him and Brittany Holmes?" Lukas asked.

"Better," Arianna said. "They found—"

"You know, Arianna," I said. "If I didn't know you better, I'd think you were gossiping."

Her cheeks turned pink. "Well, if you don't want to know what happened . . ."

But I did. So I grinned at her and said, "By all means, please continue."

"They found texts between Kip and Irving MacCormack. He's the director of the *Jolt* films. Spencer, according to those texts, MacCormack supplied Kip with the drugs."

Of course he had.

• • •

The next few weeks, I lived in my room and did nothing but physical therapy. Except one morning when Grandma drove me over to Gabe's house so I could have my first counseling session with Mr. S.

Because I was a druggie and all.

Whee.

Gabe and his sisters were in school, and Kerri was at work. So it was just me and Mr. S, hanging in his living room.

"You look well, Spencer." Mr. S said. "What would you like to talk about?"

"Did you get my letter?" Since I'd been under house arrest and Grandma had confiscated my MacBook, I'd snail-mailed

Mr. S my report on the *Jolt* movies. I'd even added the part about what Kip tried to do at his party.

"I did. I felt the report had merit and forwarded it to headquarters."

Which was a fancy way of saying, "Thanks for your trouble, we'll take it from here."

I wanted to ask a dozen more questions. But I hadn't shared the part about MacCormack claiming to be my father. And I wasn't ready to. I didn't know why. I was thinking I'd lay low until I figured out the truth about him.

"What else do you want to talk about, Spencer?"

"I don't know. Nothing. Grandma said I had to come. I came. Don't you have a list of topics or something?"

"I want to hear what's on your mind."

I took a deep breath. I had no intention of taking this seriously, but the stuff on my mind *was* serious. "Okay, fine. I want to know why all this bad stuff keeps happening. Why me? I'm a decent guy. Until Kip tricked me, I hadn't taken drugs since middle school. I didn't drink anything at that party. *And* I'm still a virgin. So why doesn't God drag Kip's life into the center ring and start taking swings at Kip's plans?"

"You're a better person than Kip. Is that what you think?" Mr. S asked.

"I know I'm a better person than Kip."

"Perhaps God knows that if he dragged Kip's life into the center ring, as you put it, Kip would be destroyed. Perhaps Kip isn't strong enough to take it. And perhaps God knows that you are a man he can use to do some good in this world. Not Kip. But you. If God *is* trying to get your attention, it's for a good reason."

"I don't want God's attention. I never asked for it. I just

want to play basketball."

"Spencer, you don't understand because you're still trying to do everything in your own power. You're strong. But no one is that strong. You've got to give your life to God. Trust him to lead you."

He meant, say the prayer. Always with the prayer with these church people. "Fine. I'll say your stupid prayer. And when nothing changes, you can tell me what to do next."

"It's not a magic spell, Spencer," Mr. S said. "It's a conversation. It's asking God to be part of your life. And it doesn't end there. It's hard work. Sometimes it sucks."

I frowned. Had Mr. S really just used the word "sucks"?

"But you'll never be alone again. And you can always ask him for help."

"I ask him for help already. I don't get help."

"So you're asking the NBA coach to put you in the game before signing the contract to play?" Mr. S asked.

That stopped me. Is that really what I was doing?

"I want you to think about that, Spencer. And when you come back next week, I want to hear what you discovered."

Uh, oh-kay.

"Why don't we talk about what happened two Saturdays ago," Mr. S said.

So I told him what I remembered. And when I started to tell him what I'd pieced together, he stopped me.

"Let's not speculate just yet. Go back a bit. You said you didn't want to go to the party. Why did you?"

"Because I said I would months ago. It was a special promotional party for the *Jolt* movies. Kip earned points or something. And even though I was ticked at him, I figured it was better than sitting home for the third day in a row, working my knee."

"Why were you angry with Kip?"

I wasn't about to tell him about Kip and Brittany. "He cheated on his girlfriend. I thought he should have broken up with her."

"But he didn't?"

"No. He was trying to have two girlfriends. I think."

"And you disapproved?"

"Wouldn't you?"

"I sense you're still angry with him."

"Yes, I'm angry! This is all his fault." And MacCormack's. My idiot "father."

"You mean the drugs."

"He risked the whole team. He risked our chance at State. I could go to jail because of him. Even if I do get my knee in shape, what college is going to want a druggie with a record? No college. And he blamed Trella for it all. He thinks he can do whatever he wants."

"So, you're judging him for his sin."

"Well, somebody should."

"That's not your place, Spencer. The Bible says God is the only judge."

"Well, what's taking him so long?"

Mr. S bit back a smile, which ticked me off. Here I was being honest, like he wanted, and he was laughing at me?

"Did you get Mary's text?" Mr. S asked.

I gritted my teeth. "I did. And I was trying to leave when the brownies were served." I *so* wish I would have left.

"Why didn't you?" Mr. S asked.

"I couldn't get to my crutches. I asked Jasmine to get them for me several times."

"You couldn't move without them?"

"I probably could have hopped to the door. And I thought about calling Kimball to help me get out."

"Yet you didn't."

"I really thought Jasmine was going to bring them to me."

"It seems to me like you're blaming others for your choices."

Was I?

"Remember what Gabe said about responsibility?" Mr. S asked.

Gabe. Like I could forget that polished little prude dude. "A man is responsible for his choices."

"So take responsibility."

Fine. I would.

REPORT NUMBER: 12

REPORT TITLE: I Take Responsibility for My Choices
SUBMITTED BY: Agent-in-Training Spencer Garmond
LOCATION: Grandma Alice's House, Pilot Point, California
DATE AND TIME: Monday, March 12, 8:14 a.m.

MY "TAKING RESPONSIBILITY" STARTED with apologizing
to my grandma.

"I was wrong to lie to you," I said one morning over a bowl
of cereal. "I shouldn't have gone to Kip's house knowing he was
having a party. And I should have left when I got Mary's text."

"You should have left the moment you saw alcohol."

But Kip's dad drank all the time when I was over there.
Not the point. "You're right. I'm sorry. I'm trying to take
responsibility for my actions."

"I appreciate that. But your friendship with Kip is over for
a while. You need some time apart. He's a bad influence."

Couldn't argue there. "Fine." I didn't really want to see
Kip, anyway. But it wasn't like I wouldn't see him at school
when I went back.

The question was: Was I going back?

• • •

Seven days into my suspension, Grandma got a letter from the school board informing her that an expulsion hearing had been scheduled for March 26, the Monday after the state basketball championship game.

Oh, come on!

How about they expel the guy who drugged us all so he could play Grand Master Daysman?

Chaz hadn't eaten any brownies, but he'd been suspended for three days for having alcohol in his system. So he was already playing again. As was Usain Bolt—I mean, Desh. But Mike and Alex had been expelled like me.

I'd been keeping tabs on the games online. I didn't have the guts to contact Coach. So far the guys were still in it. Chaz had fouled out in the last game, though—the regional semi-final. He was the only point guard on the team now. Kip could play the position long enough to give Chaz a breather, but Chaz was it. I texted him and told him awesome job and to be more careful next time.

Besides listening to the occasional playoff game online, now that I was out of school for even longer, I had nothing to do but physical therapy, physical therapy, and, well, more physical therapy.

Oh, yeah. And a pre-trial hearing.

But that went better than expected. I was certain that with my past record, the judge wouldn't believe me. But my defender had gathered statements from the partygoers. No one knew that anything had been put in the brownies. I was a victim of involuntary intoxication. As each statement was read aloud, I made a mental note to thank Jasmine for being so honest. She not only made it clear that I'd asked for my crutches repeatedly, she also admitted that Kip had asked her to stall me until I tried the brownies.

With friends like Kip, who needed enemies?

But those statement were good enough for the judge, who dismissed the charges against me.

I was free to go.

● ● ●

The following Thursday afternoon, the day after the guys had won the Regional Finals, Coach Van Buren showed up on Grandma's doorstep with a manila folder in his hand. Grandma let him in.

"Hey," I said. "What's up?"

He greeted me, then turned to Grandma. "Mrs. Garmond, certain members of the school board have banded together to make an example of Spencer. But I don't think he deserves such an honor. So, I've found a loophole."

"What kind of loophole?" she asked.

"They've been on me all year to hire a shooting coach. I've finally found the right guy. Spencer would even get paid."

Me? "Are you serious?"

He slapped down his folder onto the coffee table. "Just need you to sign this W-2."

"No," Grandma said. "I'll not see him rewarded for this."

I opened my mouth to protest, but Coach beat me to it.

"Mrs. Garmond, normally I'd agree with you a hundred percent. But I was told Spencer had no alcohol in his system. Everyone else did. It's against the law to slip someone a Mickey, and that's essentially what happened at that party. Kip is the one who should be made an example of in this, but since there's no proof, the school board is going after the other boys. I'll be testifying on Spencer's behalf at the school board hearing. And you should know that I'm very proud of this young man. He has come a long way since I've known him."

"I appreciate that, Mr. Van Buren, but I'll have to think it over."

"Thank you, ma'am. Just don't think too long."

• • •

The second part of my taking responsibility was to write an apology letter to my high school, for embarrassing them with scandal. While I was at it, I also recorded one for my YouTube channel. No sense trying to pretend this hadn't happened.

The night before the state championship final, Grandma came into my room.

"I'm going to let you go to the game with your team."

I tried to act like I didn't care. "Thank you."

"You're still grounded."

"Okay."

"There and back. I called your coach to make sure that you don't leave his sight."

"That's fair." And it was.

"I don't want you to lie to me anymore."

It was weird that she'd clamped onto lying as my biggest sin, but I guess it was one of the Ten Commandments and all.

"I'm sorry," I said again.

"You're going to have to earn my trust back."

"I know." She didn't say anything else, so I added, "Thank you, Grandma."

"I love you, Spencer, you know that right?"

"Yeah." I loved her too.

She kissed the top of my head and left, closing my door behind her.

● ● ●

Since church was the only place I saw anyone I knew, that's where Arianna, Gabe, and Lukas had been filling me in on what was going on at school. The cops had formally pressed charges against Kip for drugging everyone, but his dad hired a lawyer and made a big stink. So until Kip's pre-trial hearing—which was after the state game—the school had decided to give Kip the benefit of the doubt, which I guess meant that they thought all of us were lying about what happened.

So when I showed up at the school to get on the bus to Sacramento, Kip was there. And no one was talking to him.

It was all really weird. Like we were going to a funeral instead of a state championship basketball game. Parents and classmates had shown up to cheer us off, but it still felt . . . hopeless, I guess.

Not the best attitude to have right before a game like this.

I got on the bus and sat in the middle. Chaz sat in the seat behind mine. Kip got on next and paused as he passed my seat.

"Why are you even here?" he asked.

"I'm a coach."

"You're not *my* coach."

"I told you to wait until after state to have your dumb party."

"So this is *my* fault?"

"Duh," Chaz said.

"You drugged people, Kip," I said. "That's a felony. And you're going to get caught."

"You should be thanking me. If it wasn't for my dad, I wouldn't be here now."

"I don't care if you're here now," I said. "I'd happily trade you for Mike and Alex." But Mike and Alex were still expelled like me for eating the brownies, and since they'd been drinking at the party, Coach hadn't "hired" them to come along.

"You should care," Kip said. "We can't win without me."

That shut me up. Because I used to say the same thing. Yet our team had made it this far with me on the bench. Kip was wrong. "Yes, they can. But only if they play like a team, which means you have to stop acting like you're God."

"Why don't you go home? Your knee is shot. You're done with basketball. Get over it."

Fire kindled in my chest, but before I could reply, Coach climbed onto the bus.

"That's enough, Kip," Coach said. "I hear you talking like that again, *you'll* be done."

So Kip continued on to the back of the bus.

No one sat with him.

● ● ●

The CIF Division V State Boys Basketball Championship was being held at the Power Balance Pavilion in Sacramento. We were playing St. Joseph Notre Dame, the team that lost to Rock Academy last year. I'd been keeping track of their games online, but we'd never played them before. I really wasn't sure what to expect. Coach had showed the guys a few games, but that was before Grandma had given me permission to come, so

I hadn't seen them.

The game started out pretty even. They were good on defense; so were we. But they were tall—had three guys as tall as me but thick like Desh. Chaz messed up two drives to the basket when he came up against those trees guarding the hoop.

We really could have used Mike and Alex's help. Dan was doing his best. He had the height, but not the muscle.

They got the first basket, but Kip got one on a fast break right after. We were faster than they were, but Desh was having a hard time scoring.

With a minute ten left in the first quarter it was 8-2, their lead. Chaz tried another drive to the basket and ended up on his rear in the paint. The St. Joe's center got the rebound and lobbed it down the court to their guard for an easy lay-up.

No, no!

Coach groaned. "We need outside shooters," he told me. "They're too tall."

He was right. Chaz just didn't have the skill to go up against guys like that. And Desh and Dan couldn't do it without Mike or Alex's help.

"Chaz!" Coach held up two fingers. "Let's run two!"

That play would set Kip up to shoot a three.

Chaz nodded and brought down the ball. He ran the play and passed the ball to Kip. But Kip missed the shot and St. Joe's got the rebound.

Coach sat down beside me and sighed. "You think Jonathan can handle the pressure?"

"I don't know." I glanced down the bench to the end where three under-classmen were still wearing their warm-ups. "He can make those shots, though."

"If he makes more than one, they'll shut him down, and

then we'll have to see what else we could try. But if you're sure about him . . ."

I wasn't sure about anything, but what did we have to lose? "He hit eight out of ten from beyond the arc last time I worked with him."

"Go talk to him, then. I'll put him in second quarter."

I reached down for my crutches—forget that. I leaned forward, looked down the bench. "Jonathan!" His head popped out, and I waved him over. "Move down." I nudged Colin and all the guys slid over a seat.

Jonathan sat beside me, and I said, "Coach is putting you in at the quarter. Remember what we worked on at practice. Square up, then shoot. We need some outside shots. They don't have to be threes. Just relax and make them count, okay?"

Jonathan nodded, though he looked like he might pass out.

At the break, Coach put Jonathan in for Kip and moved Kip to play point to give Chaz a break. He told Kip to get the ball to Jonathan and see what he could do.

But when the clock started, the ball ran back and forth without much of a break. Three minutes and we still hadn't had a chance to get the ball to Jonathan.

When Kip got a rebound, Coach yelled, "Slow it down and run the play!"

But Kip took off for a fast break, even though there were already two St. Joe's trees waiting at the other end. Instead of driving for the basket, he T-ed off to the side and shot a three. A brick. St. Joe's got the rebound and everyone was running again.

Coach screamed at Kip, then sent Chaz to replace him.

When Kip came to the bench, he asked, "Why'd you take me out?"

"You can't listen, you're not going to play."

"You can't win without me," Kip said.

"Sit down," Coach said.

Kip sat.

The next time we had the ball, Chaz called play two and got the ball to Jonathan. He squared up and shot a three.

All net.

"Yes!" I started to jump up, but my knee didn't like it. So I just cheered instead. Jonathan was grinning like a kid at Disneyland.

He managed to sink one more three before St. Joe's put two guys up in his face, which left Desh wide open under the hoop.

"Pass it, Jonathan!" He needed to—

He passed it. A little short. One of the trees tipped it with his finger and sent it flying out of bounds.

"Aww, don't throw it away!" Kip yelled.

"He saw the pass, though. He saw Desh. That was good." I raised my voice. "Good try, Jon! Way to see it!"

And on we fought.

At halftime the score was 19-13. Coach wrote out a few new plays for outside shooters, and they worked on the court the first couple times. Kip and Jonathan scored. But St. Joe's defense learned quickly and put a stop to it.

With a strong defensive game on both sides, both teams quickly reached the bonus, which slowed down the clock. We matched them well from the free throw line, though, and were keeping up until Chaz fouled out.

And that was the beginning of the end. Our guys were dog

tired. And we were down by ten with a minute six left. For many coaches, that would start the "foul them on purpose" part of the game, but Coach didn't play that way.

We ran with them and played good D. Kip chased down a loose ball and scored on the fast break, bringing the final score to 46 to 38.

And that was it. Game over. We'd lost.

• • •

I stared out the window into the rising sun. We should have won state. We'd been the better team—until I'd gotten hurt and Alex and Mike had been expelled. If none of the bad stuff had happened to us, we would have won that title easily.

But maybe *better* wasn't the right word. I'd been cocky. I might have been the floor general, but Kip had always been my choice pass. I played favorites, and we won that way. But it hadn't made us a team. Despite my averaging 6.2 assists per game, I'd been a selfish player. Methodical. Knowing exactly how I wanted my endgame to look, then doing what it took to get that.

I felt bad we lost, but not for me or Kip or Mike or Alex or even Desh. I felt bad for Dan, who was a nice guy and didn't do stupid stuff. I felt bad for Jonathan, who'd tried really hard tonight. And I felt bad for Coach. It couldn't be easy coaching a bunch of jerks like us.

My Precious II bleeped, and I dug it out of my pocked to read the text. Grandma had only let me have it for the road trip, and would be taking it back the moment I stepped in the house. My pulse sped up when I saw it was from Grace.

Lost my phone cord & couldnt charge my phone. Im fine.

Dont worry. See u soon.

Soon? Did that mean she was coming back? It took me twenty miles to formulate a reply that was both kind and caring but not overly desperate.

Thanks for letting me know. We all miss you.

I stared out the window of the bus, thinking about my life and Grace and my knee and the future. As we passed by some huge fields and approached the freeway split where the 205 veered off the 5 to San Francisco, San Jose, and Oakland, I felt like that was my life, kind of a road diverged. Was I going to go my way? Or God's way?

Seemed like my way hadn't done me all that much good lately. I guessed there wasn't any real reason not to try it God's way. What was the worst that could happen? I could tear my other ACL?

Yeah, that would suck.

But I had nothing else to look forward to right now except months of physical therapy and the possible return of Grace. I didn't doubt that God existed. I just wasn't sure I bought the whole mysterious prayer thing. But maybe it was like making a promise or something. A vow. Or like swearing fealty to a lord, like a medieval knight. And if that's all it really took to stay out of hell, I'd be an idiot not to do it, right?

It certainly couldn't make matters worse.

Maybe that logic was stupid, but it made sense to me. So I hunched down in my seat and started to pray.

THE END

Spencer will return in *Broken Trust*

Come hang out with Jill!

www.JillWilliamson.com

www.facebook.com/jwilliamsonwrites

www.twitter.com/JillWilliamson

ACKNOWLEDGEMENTS

Special thanks to Mike Turrell for helping me with police procedures, to James Scott Bell for his help with court procedures, and all my NCAA basketball helpers: Grayson Leder, Patricia Woodside and son, Rebecca Luella Miller, Scott Abel, James Scott Bell, Joe Torosian, and Kourtney Leone.

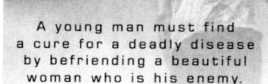

Come hang out with us!

Contests, encouragement, and community
for young writers.

www.GoTeenWriters.com
And join the community of writers on Facebook:
http://www.facebook.com/groups/goteenwriters

CPSIA information can be obtained at www.ICGtesting.com
Printed in the USA
LVOW10s1553240816

501679LV00019B/872/P